The Tail of 'Too Bad' Mike

Iain Cameron Williams

The Tail of 'Too Bad' Mike

This is the tale of Mike the skateboarding shrew and how he acquired his unusual nickname 'Too Bad'

'Too Bad' Mike ™
i will publishing
ISBN 978-1-916-14655-6
edition 2

CONTENTS

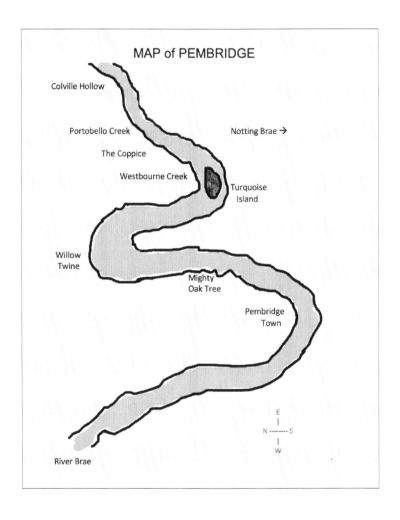

The story takes place during this year's summer solstice …

Take note, readers:

*"You are about to enter a world,
unlike any other you might know
where nothing is as it seems
and nothing seems as it is.
Tread carefully and take heed,
for there are always lessons to be learned
no matter who you might be
or how intelligent you may think you are."*

Extract from the *Pembridge Journal of Ancient Philosophy.*

The Tail of 'Too Bad' Mike

CHAPTER 1

The Curious Matter of the Missing Tail

Though it had the grandest of names, the kingdom of Pembridge was quite an ordinary place, compact in size and not in the slightest bit apparent to the human eye. Many animals believed humans had not the faintest idea of its existence. Its smallness was considered an advantage, for it kept the district exclusive and easy to govern. The residents preferred it as such. Thus, Pembridge had existed in anonymity for more years than time cared to remember.

Today began like every other summer's day, with the dawn rising high above the pencilled edge of the horizon to be welcomed by a tangerine sun as large as a baked muffin and just as warm. Among the hollows and banks of the River Brae and in the woods and meadows of Pembridge, today would surpass every day before it and unfold into an escapade the likes of which its inhabitants would never forget. Indeed, it would be transcribed into the journals of history, as the day a shrew became the most celebrated animal in the land.

Unlike all the other water shrews in the kingdom, Mike was born without a tail.

Had he been missing a leg, or an ear, or even a toe, or any other part of his small but perfectly formed anatomy, Mike may have considered himself out of the ordinary or been a little self-conscious of his appearance. As it stood, his mirror image confirmed him to be as handsome as any other shrew, so never once did such glum, morose thoughts ever enter his head. Besides, Mike was fortunate to possess one of the happiest dispositions of any animal alive. For him, every morning brought with it a new adventure waiting to be explored. As if that wasn't enough reason to feel happy, there was another significant fact why all this should be.

A few days after Mike was born, his parents died tragically in a river flood. His next of kin fell upon his grandparents from his father's side. When his grandmother Clara, a skilled seamstress, first found out about Mike's missing appendage, she set to work, making him the finest tail imaginable from woven horsehair and a skein of the hardiest black cotton thread known to tailor's. The tail would help maintain Mike's balance. When Mike was fully-grown, his grandmother presented him with the tail, and from that day onwards, Mike had worn it everywhere he went. The tail was much admired by all and the envy of every shrew in the land.

Mike was very proud of his short, slender tail. Each night before he went to bed, he would take it off and wash it meticulously in a bowl of warm soapy water before laying it neatly on a wicker tray to dry. On this fateful summer morning, Mike awoke as usual bright and early to the sound of the sparrow's call. As he curled out of bed from beneath the warm feather duvet onto the clay floor, he noticed something most peculiar. His tail was not where he thought he had left it the night before.

Mike gazed at his tailless reflection in the long, silver foil mirror beside his washbowl. "A shrew without a tail is a rare sight, indeed," Mike declared thoughtfully, as he breathed in and pushed out his chest. Mike was just as proud of his toned physique as he was of his bespoke tail.

Over the next few minutes, Mike searched every nook and cranny of his cosy lair, hunting for his missing tail - under his feather pillow, inside his lopsided wardrobe, and through all four cluttered drawers of his small matchbox chest, including the top drawer where Clive the spider slept. He even checked the outdoor washing line, but all to no avail, for no matter where he looked, Mike could not find his tail.

Puzzled by the whole sorry conundrum, Mike sat down on his favourite wooden 'thinking' stool and pondered. As much as he wanted to dismiss the thought, he couldn't help but think that something, somehow, wasn't quite right about this very curious matter.

Like a detective, Mike began to retrace his movements from the previous day.

"Perhaps I dropped it on the way home from visiting Grandfather Gus? Or maybe I lost it when I went for a swim with Harvey the trout? Or did someone craftily sneak into my burrow while I was asleep and snatch it from under my snout?"

These were imponderables Mike found impossible to answer on an empty stomach.

"I know," he said out loud, in an attempt to calm his restlessness. "I'll have breakfast."

He promptly stood up, crossed over to the shelf, and removed a loaf of crusty rye bread.

On a normal day, Mike would eat two breakfasts. Today, as he had pressing business at hand, he decided to eat only one, which is a waste of a good breakfast in anybody's book.

"Three slices of bread with raspberry jam and a pot

of dandelion tea," said Mike, gleefully. "That should perk me up."

Clive the spider, sporting a silk nightcap, suddenly poked his head out of the top drawer in the small matchbox chest to see what all the fuss was about.

"If you don't mind me saying," spoke the spider in a dry drawl, "I'd rather you didn't talk so loud. You're interrupting my sleep." From his tone, Clive sounded decidedly annoyed. "I have a lot of yarning to do today, and my energy levels are still not at their peak."

Having spoken his mind, the spider disappeared as quickly as he had appeared, back into the dark recess of the top drawer.

"How strange," thought Mike. "Clive doesn't normally fly off the handle."

This really was turning out to be a most extraordinary day.

The Tail of 'Too Bad' Mike

CHAPTER 2

The Trail of the Mystery Footprints

Mike's burrow nestled in Colville Hollow on the north bank of the River Brae. The river defined almost two-thirds of the kingdom's boundary. The waterway took its name from a remote peak sat among hills in the east. Its sparkling clear waters were unspoiled by the meddling hands of developers.

Away in the distance, but not too far away, on top of a low southern hill was the picturesque village of Notting Brae. It was a human village. Thankfully for all the animals, birds, and insects that inhabited Pembridge, most humans, most of the time, never wandered farther than their own back gardens.

After taking breakfast, Mike decided to pay his grandfather a visit, to see if he could shed any light on the subject of his missing tail.

Ever since his grandmother Clara passed away peacefully in her sleep during last winter's long cold spell, when the ground turned as hard as toffee, and the river froze over for days, Grandfather Gus vowed the time had finally arrived for him to find a more sheltered home to retire to. With the last rites of winter and the blessing of spring, Grandfather Gus packed up his belongings. He moved into the warmer surroundings of an old houseboat that occasionally got infested with humans. The boat was moored nearby at Portobello Creek on the River Brae.

Some days his grandfather suffered from bouts of intestinal wind. Mike hoped today would not be one of those blustery occasions. On Mike's last visit, his grandfather's flatulence had been so acute it had blown Mike across the deck from one side to the other.

Before setting out, Mike brushed his teeth with arrowroot paste. He then shaped his short mohawk into style with a dollop of Cuckoo Spit gel until it was as taut as the bristles on a paintbrush. With his skateboard and favourite denim jacket packed inside his backpack, Mike headed off.

It was a short walk to Portobello Creek. As the weather that morning was so pleasant, Mike decided to take the long route, walking backward, to retrace his footsteps from the previous day. By the time he arrived at the creek, it had taken him an extra five minutes.

"Time well spent," thought Mike, for during the walk, he had discovered something most interesting - a fresh set of shrew footprints that did not belong to him. They led all the way from his front garden along the riverbank. At the creek, the mystery footprints continued further along the riverside as if they were heading to the coppice.

What made the footprints so intriguing was the distinctive indentation of the right forefoot, which had four narrow clawed toes. Everybody knows, unlike a mouse that has four toes on its front feet and five on its hind, shrews have five clawed toes on all four feet.

Mike peered across the river at his grandfather's houseboat.

"Good," he remarked in a cheerful voice. "No humans about."

He could see his grandfather asleep in a hammock on the deck.

"Good morning, Grandad," hollered Mike.

Grandfather Gus bolted upright, rubbed the sleep from his eyes, then squinted inquisitively across at the riverbank. Without warning, he let fly an almighty fart that swayed his hammock perilously back and forth before thrusting him through the air like a discarded cabbage. He came to an abrupt halt beside the starboard rail, with his hind legs dangling precariously over the edge of the vessel.

"I thought I'd warned you not to disturb me when I'm asleep," growled Grandfather Gus in his grumpiest voice.

"Sorry, Grandad," apologized Mike, "but I've got something important to ask you."

"That's all very well for you to say," grumbled Grandfather Gus, as he straightened his posture and flicked dust from the sleeve of the long nightshirt he was wearing. "Please tell. What is so important that you have to interrupt my early, early morning snooze?"

"I've lost my tail and wondered if you'd seen it? I know I had it with me when I visited you yesterday, but when I woke up this morning, it had vanished."

"How strange!" said Grandfather Gus as he shook his head from side to side. "How very strange, indeed. I don't recall seeing you yesterday."

Mike knew his grandfather was a little forgetful at times, but surely not that forgetful!

"How very unsatisfactory, my dear boy," his grandfather continued. "A shrew without a tail is like … a yacht without a sail. We must find it at once."

As if by coincidence, but clearly it wasn't, Harvey the trout popped his head out of the water to see what all the bother was about. From his overtly stern expression, it was apparent that he, too, had got out of bed on the wrong side this morning.

"Good morning, Harvey," Mike called out. "I've lost my tail. Have you seen it on your travels?"

Harvey stared at Mike with a cold, vacant air about him. "I can't say I have, so I won't. But I'll keep one eye open, just in case."

Harvey was a cantankerous, nosey, brown trout that didn't like being disturbed, especially in his own backwater. However, his curiosity got the better of him. He swam a little closer towards the bank to get a more advantageous look at Mike's tailless behind.

"Too bad, Mike, about losing your tail," carped the trout, dryly, swishing his rudder from one side to the other. "A shrew without a tail is like … an ocean without a whale."

With that said, Harvey disappeared back down to the riverbed.

"Surely, someone must know where my tail is!" exclaimed Mike, despondently.

Grandfather Gus did the one thing he could always be relied upon to do at a time like this, he broke wind. The force was so powerful it blew him straight off the boat into the river. He hit the water with such a splash, Harvey the trout poked his head back out to see what had happened.

"That's me washed for today," joked Grandfather Gus, as he paddled his tiny forefeet in a circular motion. Without ceremony, he then let out another enormous trump.

Mike laughed and laughed until his stomach ached, for it was the funniest thing he'd seen all day. A large bubble had become trapped inside his grandfather's nightshirt and caused it to inflate like a balloon.

"Too bad, Mike ... about losing your tail," reiterated his grandfather, as he struggled to unfasten the top button on his nightshirt to release the air. "As soon ... as I get ... this shirt off," he finally undid the button. "Ah! That's better," he sighed, as his shirt slowly began to deflate, "I'll finish bathing, then put on my 'thinking' cap and see what I can come up with."

"Okay, Grandad," nodded Mike, "but don't take long. I need to be off soon. I've got a trail to follow and a tail to find."

Mike was in a rush to get away before the heat from the morning sun became too unbearable underfoot, which was one of the reasons he'd brought his skateboard along, so he could ride it some of the way.

After bathing, Grandfather Gus climbed the rope ladder back onboard the houseboat. He shook the water from his fur and towelled himself dry, put on a clean shirt, then leaned back into his canvas hammock and did as he had promised and put on his 'thinking' cap.

Mike remained on the riverbank, watching the playful water currents in the river teasing the curled pondweed. The sight of the small yellow flowers on the tips of the weeds made him feel quite peckish all of a sudden. He dipped a paw into the water and snapped off a couple of flower heads to munch. The flowers jogged his memory of an old fishwives tale, well, more of a rhyming remedy, which he recited to amuse himself.

"A twist of lemon zest
in a cup of hot water
works wonders for wind
on your son or your daughter."

"I hope that little ditty wasn't directed at me!" interrupted Harvey, offhandedly.

"Oh! Harvey. I'd forgotten you were there," Mike replied, tactfully.

"I see Grandfather Gus is in fine form on this bright morn," smirked Harvey, rather pompously. "Perhaps you should offer him that snippet of sage advice. While I'm here, may I regale you with my thoughts on the subject of your missing appendage?"

"If you must," answered Mike reluctantly.

"Then allow me to proceed."

Harvey smugly applied more glide to his rudder and swam over to the riverside, where he came to a halt directly in front of Mike.

"You forget, my dear friend ... I have periscopic vision ... and as such, I can see everything that goes on, both in and alongside the river."

Harvey was a smart, conniving old trout. He knew exactly how to hold someone's attention by saying just enough to keep them interested without divulging the full story.

"There's a shrew that lives to the west in Pembridge Town. Although I'm not one to spread gossip," he coughed politely, "but what else are you supposed to do with it? Rumour has it he has two tails, and that's a sure way of attracting the young females. I believe it's all the fashion on that side of town. His name is Handsome Cad ... he's a bit of a Jack-the-lad. His best mate is Spiv, a jack of all trades. Spiv sells counterfeit goods from a market stall in Pembridge Square, but I'm not one to blabber you must understand."

Harvey let Mike ponder on this salacious piece of hearsay for a moment before letting out a loud, cavernous yawn.

"Time for a snooze," said Harvey, drowsily, as he slowly slid out of sight beneath the temperate, silvery-blue water, leaving Mike on the grass bank with a whole new kettle of fishy tales to contemplate.

Rocking back and forth in his canvas hammock wearing his 'thinking' cap certainly had the desired effect upon Grandfather Gus, for it wasn't long before he came up with an inspired plan.

"If I attach some string where Mike's tail should be, nobody will know the difference!"

With great enthusiasm, Grandfather Gus set about making his grandson a new tail. This he made from a length of discarded fisherman's twine, which he cut to size. When he'd completed the task, he tied it to a twig, then called out to Mike on the riverbank.

"Attach this to your backside with some extra strong Samson snail glue."

Grandfather Gus flung the twig ashore. Mike unfastened the string, grabbed a passing Samson snail, then slapped a large dollop of snail glue on his rear.

"That should do the trick and stick," chuckled Grandfather Gus.

"How clever was Grandad," thought Mike as he secured the string to his furry behind.

Unable to contain his curiosity, Mike peered down at his reflection in the river.

"It may only be temporary, but it looks almost real," Grandfather Gus assured his grandson.

"You always have a habit of coming up trumps, Grandad, but this time you've exceeded yourself."

"I do! Do I?" Grandfather Gus coughed bashfully before quickly recovering his composure.

"In truth, I do, my boy. That's why they call me a 'wise' old shrew."

"Grandad, it's time I was making a move. The sun is rising higher than a baked muffin, and my stomach is feeling peckish."

Before Grandfather Gus bid his grandson farewell, he offered him one further word of advice.

"Whatever you do, dear boy ... do not get your new tail wet. Otherwise, it will fray, and if it frays, you'll have to go and see Mr Stitch, the tailor, over in Willow Twine. Just mention my name. I'm sure he'll be more than happy to make you a proper tail."

Mike wished his grandfather goodbye and set off.

Just as he was departing, Harvey, the trout, poked his head back out of the water.

"Well," said Harvey, doubtfully. "It may fool those that live among us who are long-sighted, but it clearly looks like a piece of old string to me."

Mike was too far away to hear Harvey's snide remark, but perhaps that was the reason why he said it because he knew Mike was out of earshot. You see,

Harvey really wasn't as bad-tempered as everyone made him out to be.

The Tail of 'Too Bad' Mike

CHAPTER 3

The Queen's Constitutional

With his temporary tail attached firmly to his behind and with a puzzling set of tales to contemplate, Mike headed off, walking backward along the riverbank towards the coppice following the mystery footprints.

There was, thought Mike, something strange about what Harvey had said to him. It was as if he knew more than he was letting on, Pembridge Town, two tails, Handsome Cad? Or perhaps it had something to do with the fact that the mystery footprints, by coincidence, seemed to be leading him in exactly the same direction!

Mike couldn't quite work it out.

The river appeared calm and unexciting that morning. Yet beneath its tranquil surface lived an unimaginable world of challenge and spectacle, where nothing remained constant except the measured flow of the water.

Mike enjoyed eating out. He had a voracious appetite and would generally spend a good part of the day foraging for food. He knew there would be many eateries to snack in along the way. Unusually for a water shrew, Mike was a vegetarian. That said, he did eat the occasional crustacean, especially river shrimp, if there was no vegetation to gorge on. By the time he reached the coppice, he'd eaten a wide variety of leaves, various nuts and seeds, and enough berries to make a plump summer pudding.

However, the walk did not pass without incident.

About twenty minutes along the route, just before the bluebell patch in the coppice, Mike accidentally bumped into the stem of a tall, pink snapdragon. Half-hidden inside one of the dragon's heads diligently rummaging for nectar was a very industrious bumblebee.

It was unusual to see a bumblebee up so early at this time of the day. This particular one was far too busy collecting pollen to notice a shrew walking backward. The collision came like a bolt out of the blue for them both, causing the bee to lose its balance and slip feet first out of the velvety mouth of the dragon's head. The bee tumbled to the ground with a dull thud, landing flat on his back in a cloud of

en, a position a bee finds immensely tricky to get
up from.

ike was so taken aback by the commotion, he did
immediate about-face turn to see what had
ppened. On the ground in front of him was the
st bizarrely dressed bumblebee he had ever seen,
wearing a flight jacket decorated with a row of five
impressive Royal Air Force medals, construing tales
of heroism.

"Now, what have I done!" exclaimed Mike,
anxiously.

As the pollen cloud slowly dispersed, the bee began
to look worse and worse. Each of its six legs pointed
upright in the air.

"Allow me to help," offered Mike, in earnest.

The bee did not respond.

"Yikes!" uttered Mike, with a look of growing
concern. "A hit to the head ... this could be serious ...
I hope he's not dead."

Mike leaned over and gently prodded the bee in the
chest.

Slowly, like an automated toy being wound up, the
bee came to life. First, its eyes blinked, then it sprang
to his feet, and his four wings began to unfold. Next,
its engine buzzed into action. Round and round, the
bee spun, like a demented firecracker, in ever-
increasing circles. Then, as quick as a wink, the bee

gathered speed and rose into the air where it ho in front of Mike's face.

The look of relief in Mike's expression immediate.

"Wing Commander Hari Ha-ha here, sir .. who, if I may be so bold as to ask, are you?" aske bumblebee.

Wing Commander Hari Ha-ha was a veteran of the Pembridge Royal Air Force and one of its most distinguished and charismatic fighter pilots, having achieved 'ace' status during the Pollen War after shooting down five enemy aircraft in one day. Though his days of combat had long since passed, due to his great age and rickety legs, his loyalty to the realm remained steadfast.

"Mike's my name, but more to the point, how are you feeling?"

"Tricky question, that one, sir," answered the Wing Commander. "Very tricky."

The bumblebee flexed his leg joints to check they were in working order.

"All present and correct, sir," he confirmed, as he hovered stiffly to attention in mid-air and gave Mike a military salute.

"I'm relieved to hear," replied Mike. "For a nasty moment, I thought you were dead!"

"Dead! What! Me, sir?"

A look of surprise flashed across the Wing Commander's face.

"Just laying low, sir … an old trick I learned in the Air Force to fool the enemy."

Although Mike found the eccentric Wing Commander fascinating to talk to, he found the formalities a tad irritating.

"You certainly had me fooled."

"It works every time, sir."

"So, I see."

The bee gave a cursory glance over Mike's shoulder and then discreetly whispered, "I don't mean to alarm you, sir, but there's a piece of old string following you around."

"That's not string,' Mike corrected the bee. 'It's my temporary tail. You see, I've lost mine, and I'm on a mission to find it."

"A mission! That sounds jolly exciting. You can trust me. I won't tell a soul."

Seconds later, a shrill fanfare of trumpets filled the morning air. Mike and the Wing Commander turned to see where the sound was coming from. Approaching was the town crier - a portly water rat. Clad in a black tricorn hat with a white feather attached, a crimson and gold robe, white breeches, and shiny black boots, he rang a handbell to summon attention.

"Oyez, Oyez, Oyez! All bow in the presence of beauty."

A few yards behind marched trumpeters from the royal military guard, who were blowing their horns to signal the approaching royal procession. The musicians were all female horntails, handpicked because they were ambidextrous and good at blowing their own trumpet. All were attired in state dress, and their silvery-white trumpet lilies bore the royal crest of Pembridge.

A division of the Royal Guard advanced on foot directly behind the trumpeters. The guards were drone bees, chosen for their brawny physique and stature. Some carried extended poles across their shoulders upon which rested a platform. The platform held a throne as large as a daybed, elaborately decorated with ferns, leaves, golden petals, and a white muslin canopy. Though partially hidden from view by the awning, recumbent upon it was Her Majesty Queen Beetrice II, queen bee and reigning monarch of the House of Pembridge. The picturesque procession took place most days, weather permitting. The Queen was carried for the entire route, from her castle and back.

As the procession drew closer, a crescendo of music filled the morning air. All the animals, birds, and insects stopped what they were doing, scurried out of their secret places, and lined the path to witness the spectacle.

"Oyez, Oyez, Oyez! All bow in the presence of beauty," proclaimed the town crier, yet again.

Wing Commander Hari Ha-ha signalled to Mike to lower his head.

"When the procession passes, bow your head. Whatever you do," he urged, harshly, "do not look at the Queen. Is that clear?"

"Yes ... but why?" replied Mike, sounding puzzled.

"It's the law. Superstition has it that if anyone should look at Her Majesty, her beauty will fade instantly, forever."

It was unusual for the sedentary Queen to be taking her constitutional so early in the day. She usually took it in the afternoon. There was, however, a simple explanation why today was different. The Queen was expected back in Pembridge Town by midday to perform an official duty, the opening of the summer fête. The fête was the highlight of the social calendar, and everybody who was anybody would be attending.

Renowned throughout the kingdom for her incomparable beauty and slender figure, Queen Beetrice had remained an enigmatic figure since the day she was crowned. Wherever she travelled, her humble subjects would faithfully line the lanes and pathways to pay their respect. For them, she was the bringer of joy, and all who bowed in her presence were blessed with happiness.

Although Pembridge had officially been recognized throughout history as a kingdom, surprisingly, no king had ever reigned. Only a long succession of ancestrally related Queen's had ruled.

During her lengthy reign, the current Queen had grown weary of all the fuss and adoration bestowed upon her. With very little to do all day except recline upon her throne, she found her official duties tedious. It was claimed, a smile from the Queen was as rare as the opening of a green letterbox. To hide her unhappiness, she had taken to wearing a lace veil draped loosely around her face. From behind this disguise, she could conceal her boredom and do the one thing she enjoyed more than anything else in the world, snacking between meals.

As was usual during the Queen's constitutionals, walking three steps behind the throne was the evil Lord and Lady Muck. They were mere commoners, regular bees that had risen to exalted heights and pocketed immense riches through their devious and wicked ways. Both were beaten at birth with the ugly stick and were prone to over-exaggerate their gestures and apparel to disguise their hideousness. Their position in the hierarchy afforded them all the

neither attractive nor slim. Her face resembled a brown leather rugby ball, and her body was the size of a layered chocolate cake, with all the trimmings.

As a result of the Queen's sweet tooth, her once slim figure had now outgrown its memory. She had become grossly overweight. Although all the inhabitants who lived at Hive Castle knew this, nobody dared mention it for fear of being tried for treason. Her pitiful condition now meant she could fly only short distances. Hence, why she was shuttled around her kingdom, lounging inelegantly upon her golden throne.

There was, however, another lesser-known reason why the Queen had become incapacitated. She suffered from a rare condition called 'heavy legs,' an ailment her distant exiled relatives in France were extremely susceptible to. Apparently, or so Dr Quack knowledgeably informed her, it had something to do with particular climatic conditions attacking her leg joints. Entirely what those weather conditions were, nobody at the meteorological office could explain. On such days, she would lounge lethargically upon her throne, bedbound for hours without moving a single muscle … aside from her chocolate plucking claw. As for a cure, the doctor had two shelves of remedies to choose from, but none of them appeared to be effective.

Lord and Lady Muck had taken thorough advantage of such sensitive knowledge. They believed implicitly that as long as they perpetuated the belief of Her Majesty's beauty, they would remain in favour. Subsequently, they continued to wield great power and influence over the kingdom.

The procession came to an abrupt halt.

Lord Muck promptly ordered the Royal Guard to ensure all the spectators' heads remained bowed respectfully until Her Majesty regained her composure. The glum-faced Queen seemed most put out by this sudden diversion. So much so, she raised her frosty gaze from the luxurious box of chocolates she'd been delving into to take a look around her. After the guards had ascertained everything was in order, Lord Muck ordered the procession onwards. Only then did Queen Beetrice wrap her veil back around her face. Thereby enabling her to resume eating her favourite lavender chocolates.

Fortunately for Mike, Lady Luck must have been watching over him, for none of the guards observed his stolen glimpse of the Queen. However, one member of the procession did notice ... but that citizen's name shall remain secret for the time being.

An air of normality quickly resumed once the procession had passed by.

"I can't hover here nattering all day, sir," the Wing

Commander huffed, as he straightened the line of medals pinned upon his flight jacket. "I have work to do."

The monarch's presence had clearly recharged his batteries. The Wing Commander was raring to go and seemed to have forgotten entirely about his little accident from earlier on.

"I might be a humble bee, but I'm a busy bee. There's fresh sweet pollen to collect for Her Majesty." He straightened his posture, "It really is too bad Mike that you've lost your tail. A shrew without a tail is like ... a valley without a trail."

"Before you go," asked Mike hastily. "Where was the procession heading?"

"Ah! That's an easy question to answer. Today is the day the summer fête is held at Pembridge Town, and everybody will be there, including me. That's if I get my wings on and complete my duties."

Without so much as a by-your-leave, the Wing Commander ascended into the bright clear sky where he hovered momentarily before flying off.

Pembridge's summer fête took on a sudden fascination with Mike. It seemed to him that the whole neighbourhood would be in attendance, apart from Grandfather Gus. He had long since given up socializing due to his tendency to nod off at inappropriate times.

After the Wing Commander had flown off, Mike resumed his investigative trail in pursuit of the mystery footprints. At this point, Mike decided it would probably be safer if he were to stop walking backward to prevent him from bumping into any further trouble.

It was at this section of the coppice that the footprints veered away into the bluebell patch. Luckily, this was also a short cut to both Westbourne Creek and Turquoise Island, a route Mike took when visiting his best friend Wriggler, a small earthworm. It was also part of the course to Pembridge Town along the northern banks of the river.

It was here the mystery trail became less clear and far more challenging to detect. Mike's small beady eyes persevered as he weaved his way through the mass of bluebell stalks, undergrowth, and foliage.

His persistence and tracking skills paid off. It wasn't long before he'd manoeuvred his way back into the open sunlight on the western edge of the coppice, where it adjoined Westbourne Creek alongside the River Brae.

CHAPTER 4

Turquoise Island

Turquoise Island was pebble-shaped and named after the abundance of flowers that grew on it. The island had no lanes, no paths, and all the trees leaned in the same direction. It was also uninhabited by humans, making it a great place for animals to live. However, its picturesque setting and array of flora did attract the occasional human picnickers from nearby Notting Brae.

When the river was low, the northern side of the island was easy to access by foot along a naturally occurring ridge that looked a little like a hog's back. This connected the island to the mainland at Westbourne Creek.

With heavy rain, the River Brae became swollen. At such times, the water would flow rapidly on both sides of the island, leaving it wholly inaccessible to visitors on foot. Mike often visited the island to see his best friend, Wriggler. If the water level was high, he'd swim across, which could be quite hazardous if there was a strong undercurrent.

At Westbourne Creek, the mystery footprints led off in the direction of the old towpath. As the sun was rising and time was pushing on, Mike decided to break his journey and pay Wriggler a visit on Turquoise Island.

Today the river was lower than it had been for a couple of weeks, and the ridge was clearly visible. Mike always found the river less exciting when the water level was low. The bank was narrow and slippery with moss, so Mike trod warily. Halfway across, he slipped on a pebble and lost his balance, which sent him tumbling belly first into the river. Luckily, his backpack kept him afloat. He grabbed a protruding root, and gingerly hawked himself out of the water, and scuttled back up on to the ridge. The fall had shaken him a little. It took him a good few seconds to gather his wits before proceeding along to the island.

Wriggler was not an easy friend to locate. He resided in a labyrinth of soil tunnels beneath the ground. Mike's usual procedure was to holler down the first wormhole he came across.

"HELLO! ... ANYBODY HOME?"

Mike pressed his ear against the earth hole and waited for a reply.

Almost immediately, a worm pushed its head up through another wormhole and did a 360-degree turn.

"Over here, in Schwarzschild," hollered Wriggler, as he nuzzled his body further out of the hole.

Wriggler had named his tunnels, like streets. His favourite was Schwarzschild, named after the German physicist and astronomer Karl Schwarzschild who discovered black holes and wormholes. Wriggler greatly admired him.

"Oh! It's you," wheezed Wriggler. "I should have known it was you. How could I have thought it would have been anybody else but you? It's always you that interrupts me when I'm tunnelling!"

Wriggler held his head aloft towards the clear, endless, blue sky, whose colour appeared more intense than a field of cornflowers.

"I thought you might like to go skateboarding along the old towpath," said Mike, yanking his skateboard out of his backpack.

Wriggler seemed totally preoccupied with other things, mainly the weather forecast, and ignored the question. There were no clouds in the sky as far as the horizon, not even small ones. The idea of skateboarding on such a hot day as today was the furthest thing on the worm's mind.

"There's a drought on the way. I'll be dead in a

week!" shrieked Wriggler rather hysterically, as he surveyed the sky for rain clouds.

Sure, the weather that morning was particularly pleasant. There was certainly no threat of rain, but that didn't necessarily mean there was a drought on the way.

"Where did you hear such foreboding news?" asked Mike.

"Yesterday, on the radio ... humans ... they were picnicking on the island, and I overheard it on their radio."

Mike had heard the radio talking on his grandfather's houseboat and could never figure out how so many humans could squeeze themselves into such a small box.

"The radio announcer said, 'keep listening for the latest progress on the weather forecast.'"

That sounded feasible enough, thought Mike.

"So, what is this thing called 'progress'?" asked Wriggler, "and where can I find some?"

Mike was stuck for a reply.

"Perhaps that's something you should ask Grandfather Gus. I'm sure he'd know all about progress."

Wriggler said something indistinct through a mouth full of soil and then rolled over on his back ... or was it his front? Either way, he looked as if he was about to start burrowing another hole.

Wriggler really wasn't interested in making flippant conversation today. He had far more important things to concentrate on, the weather forecast, being one of them.

"I know this might sound selfish," confessed Wriggler, "but, if I don't tunnel down to the water's edge, I'll be as dry as a dried prune on the end of a spoon."

Mike was beginning to think his visit to see Wriggler wasn't such a good idea after all.

Although Mike lived in a burrow, it wasn't technically buried beneath the ground; it was a naturally occurring hole set in the side of a clay embankment. This gave it the benefit of remaining dry and warm in winter yet cool and shaded in the summer. Mike fully understood Wriggler's concern about dehydration.

"Perhaps I should go," said Mike, "and come back another time when it's not so warm, and you're not so tied up with things."

Mike sat down on the grass and packed his skateboard back into his backpack. "Oh! I forgot to mention, I've lost my tail."

Wriggler remained silent for a few moments as if to thoroughly digest that last piece of information. He seemed quite perplexed at the thought of losing one's tail. "If I lost mine, there'd be nothing left of me," joked Wriggler.

Mike thought that was very amusing and fell back laughing.

"I'm glad you found that so funny," said Wriggler, in a voice conveying very little joy.

Wriggler really did have a sense of humour, even though it appeared to be in short supply today.

"It's too bad, Mike, that you've lost your tail. A shrew without a tail is like … winter without hail." As an afterthought, he enquired, "what have you got attached to your rear?"

"It's only temporary … until I find my tail."

"But why choose a squirrel's tail?"

Mike promptly stood up and turned his head and peered down at his tail. His dip in the river had unravelled the string. He now had a bushy tail.

"I told you," smirked Wriggler. "Friends don't lie, especially not I." Then, without any warning, Wriggler slithered out of sight down his wormhole.

Mike recalled his grandfather's caution, not to get the string wet. "It seems I will have to visit Mr Stitch after all."

As if to reconfirm the fact, Mike's tail then came unstuck and flopped to the ground.

At that precise moment, Wriggler pushed his head out of a completely different wormhole to see what was going on. Something strange happened next.

Just beyond Wriggler, through a hole on the top of a curved mound, emerged a small empty dandelion and burdock bottle, seemingly on its own accord. When the bottle was clear, it toppled over and rolled down the bank.

Through the same hole, poked the pink snout of Wriggler's next hole neighbour, Belinda Bellerica, a mole, followed by her curvaceous body. Belinda was rarely seen in daylight as she spent most of her time underground. From the size of her swollen stomach, she looked heavily expectant. Belinda fluttered her thick, black eyelashes at Mike, who immediately became quite bashful.

"Did I hear you mention, Mr Stitch?" asked Belinda, sweetly, whose face was smeared with mud.

"I did," answered Mike, who couldn't stop staring at the mud on Belinda's face.

Belinda picked up on Mike's curiosity. "It's a mudpack ... good for the complexion. It contains fuller's earth."

Mike was still none the wiser. He continued, "I've lost my tail, and my grandad made me a temporary one, but now that's had it, I'll have to have a new one made."

It all sounded very confusing to Belinda.

Mike picked up the sorry piece of string to show

her.

Wriggler appeared relatively calm all of a sudden. "As you're going that way, you can take me with you. I need to get some provisions. Belinda ... as you can see, is a bit hole bound at the moment, so can't run any errands for me."

Belinda was a newcomer to the island, having only recently arrived from distant shores. Since her arrival, Wriggler had become extremely fond of her. He allowed her to reside in one of his prized holes, Einstein hole, named after Albert, for which he charged a very reasonable rent.

"Hop inside my pouch," joked Mike, knowing full well Wriggler couldn't hop into anything.

Wriggler was not amused. "Just put some soil in your pouch and lift me up."

Mike did as Wriggler suggested, then gently lifted him up and placed him inside the top pouch of his backpack.

"Too bad, Mike, about you losing your tail," called out Belinda. "A shrew without a tail is like ... a well without a pail. And could you fill the burdock bottle with water for me?" urged Belinda, still fluttering her long lashes.

"I'll drop it off on my way back," said Mike, as he made his way off.

Mike picked up the dandelion and burdock bottle

by the water's edge, filled it with water, and placed it in his backpack.

"By the way," said Mike to Wriggler, "I've decided to go to the fête at Pembridge Town after we've visited Mr Stitch. I hope you don't mind?"

Wriggler didn't mind; he'd never been to a fête before, or Pembridge Town, so he had no idea of what to expect. Besides, it sounded far more exciting than digging holes all day.

Wriggler snuggled into the soil inside Mike's pouch and poked his head out of the top, so he could enjoy the view along the way.

The Tail of 'Too Bad' Mike

CHAPTER 5

The Tailor's Holt

The Tailor's Holt wasn't too far from Turquoise Island, a few stones skim away on the next river bend. Mike returned to Westbourne Creek and cut through a short section of the wooded coppice to reach it. Wriggler had never liked the coppice. He found it cold and shady. As long as Wriggler was inside Mike's pouch, he felt safe.

Although inconvenient, the diversion wouldn't cause much delay. Mike could rejoin the trail of the mystery footprints and forage for more food along the way.

Five minutes later, Mike arrived outside the Tailor's Holt at Willow Twine on the curve of the river, where a sweeping row of weeping willow trees stood.

The Holt was situated among the bulbous roots of the tallest willow tree. The willow had a name, Gantree.

Gantree had been a loyal friend and protector of the

elderly Mr Stitch since the tailor first moved to Willow Twine. It was here Mr Stitch had made his home and opened his small bespoke tailor's shop.

Nailed on the shop's front door was a notice written in black ink informing customers of the opening times. Mike read the note carefully.

OPENING HOURS
Monday to Friday 9:12 a.m. until 11:59 a.m.
CLOSED for a very long lunch
Reopen 2:01 p.m. until 5:29 p.m.
CLOSED for very long weekends

It was signed at the bottom with a flourish of the paw ... Mr Stitch

Mike peered through the window at the large circular clock inside the shop. Somewhat peculiarly, all the numbers on its face were jumbled up. He thought it said forty-three minutes to twelve but couldn't be sure. He tried to figure out if the time on the clock fitted in with the allotted times on the notice but became so confused, he gave up. Instead, he looked back through the window to see if he could see anyone.

"That's lucky," said Mike. He could see someone inside. "The shop must be open."

From out of the blue came a loud, deep, hollow voice. "I know, tell me about it."

The voice resonated among the willow trees and startled Mike and Wriggler.

Mike turned to see who had spoken, but nobody was about. Only the motion of the hanging willow branches stirred gently in the breeze.

Wriggler felt sure it was a bad omen and got so spooked he buried his head under the soil inside the pouch he was in.

Mike gazed up into the dark thicket of drooping branches to see if a bird or animal was lurking but saw nothing out of the ordinary.

"A trick of the wind," he thought as if to dismiss it. There seemed little point in hanging around. He had more impending things to sort out.

Mike pushed the shop door open and entered to the sound of a jangling bell. Sitting behind a wooden counter at the rear of the shop was a small, elderly otter, the proprietor, Mr Stitch. He was busy repairing a torn seam on a garment. Upon the counter were rolls of smart fabric, different coloured cotton reels, and several piles of clothes patterns.

"Good day, Mr Stitch," said Mike.

The otter seemed totally engrossed in his work and appeared not to hear.

Mike gave out a loud cough to clear his throat and

tried again.

"I'm sorry to interrupt, Mr Stitch, but I see from your notice you're open for business." Mike hoped he'd got the correct time from the clock.

The otter snipped the cotton thread he was using with a small pair of scissors then peered over his half-rimmed spectacles.

"And a good day to you, sir. How may I be of assistance?"

The otter spoke in a refined, educated manner as if his larynx was coated in rich, dark chocolate.

"I've lost my tail and was hoping you could make me a new one. My grandad, who lives at Portobello Creek, told me to visit you and said I was to mention his name ... Grandfather Gus."

The otter seemed quite taken aback. As capable as he was, Mr Stitch had never before been asked, throughout his long career as a tailor, to make a tail.

There followed a measured silence. This was a usual occurrence for Mr Stitch for he always took his time considering new commissions.

"Hmmm ... I know your grandfather well, and an honourable shrew he is too. And what may I ask is your name, dear boy?"

"Mike."

There followed another measured silence as Mr Stitch unravelled a cloth tape measure.

Mike wondered if possibly he'd offended him somehow with his unusual request.

"I'm a bespoke tailor," continued the otter. "I make the finest apparel in the land, and you ask me if I can make a tail?"

It appeared Mr Stitch was slightly affronted by Mike's peculiar order.

"Yes," answered Mike uneasily. "I did."

"Hmmm ... I've been asked to make a few peculiar garments during my career as a tailor, but never a TAIL!"

There followed another long pause in the conversation. Wriggler poked his head out of the backpack pouch to find out what was causing the delay. At this rate, their chat could take a while. To speed things up, Mike turned and showed Mr Stitch his tailless behind. Wriggler shot out of sight back inside the pouch.

There followed another considered silence.

"Hmmm ... not an agreeable sight," mumbled the otter under his breath.

Mr Stitch was a fastidious otter and really didn't like things to look untidy or out of place. He could see clearly the work that was required to remedy Mike's predicament. However, there was one slight problem, something he couldn't rectify at that moment in time. While mulling over his options, the tailor came up with an alternative solution.

"Too bad, Mike, to hear you've lost your tail. Why, a shrew without a tail is like … a hammer without a nail," expressed the otter rather eloquently. "Leave it with me. I'm sure I can string something together."

Mike was thrilled with the response but a little confused about what Mr Stitch wanted him to leave behind.

This he asked.

"No! No!" chuckled the tailor. "There's no need to leave your behind, behind," he assured Mike. "By all means, take it with you. A standard size tail is a standard size tail on anybody's notepad."

The otter jotted down '1 standard size tail' upon his notepad.

"When can I collect it?" asked Mike keenly.

Mr Stitch thought long and hard as if he was adding up the time it would take to make such a tail. Eventually, he replied.

"If I've got my sums correct, twenty-three minutes past one … and don't be late. I'll make it during my lunch as I'm closed this afternoon as it's the summer fête over at Pembridge Town and I have to buy some much-needed black thread from the market."

This was splendid news. It gave Mike time to grab lunch and go skateboarding with Wriggler along the old towpath along Willow Twine, where it hadn't become overgrown with weeds and rambling ivy.

"That'll suit me perfectly, Mr Stitch, for I too intend to visit the summer fête as I also have important matters to attend to."

To all intent and purposes, it seemed everyone was happy with the arrangement. Mike bid the otter a temporary farewell and took off in the direction of the towpath, with Wriggler's head perched happily back over the rim of the backpack pouch.

At precisely thirty seconds before twenty-three minutes past one, Mike entered the tailor's shop to the sound of the jangling doorbell. Mr Stitch was sitting behind the long, wooden counter at the rear of the shop. He snipped the cotton thread he was holding, then placed the small pair of scissors on the counter. The otter peered over the top of his half-rimmed spectacles to see who had entered.

"Hello again, Mr Stitch. I hope I'm not too early?"

Mr Stitch gazed across at the large clock on the wall and watched as the small second hand moved ever closer towards the number twelve. As soon as it reached the dozen, the otter spoke.

"You cut that fine."

Mike placed his backpack upon the counter in

preparation for the fitting. Wriggler poked his head over the rim of the pouch so he could get a prime view.

From beneath the counter, the otter produced the tail. Mike and Wriggler stared in disbelief.

"It's RED!" exclaimed Mike.

"Bright RED!" shrieked Wriggler.

Mr Stitch proudly straightened the tail out to show the full effect.

"Poppy-coloured," explained Mr Stitch, "made from the finest silk thread in the kingdom. It's been soaked in starch for several minutes to stiffen its shape, but it's still got flexibility."

"But it's RED!" exclaimed Mike, again.

"Bright RED!" echoed Wriggler.

"Don't vex about the shade. The colour will fade once the sun's rays hit it," Mr Stitch assured Mike. "I'm sure you'll be the talk of the fête and much admired by all."

"But it's RED!" Mike shuddered.

"It's definitely RED!" agreed Wriggler.

The otter appeared increasingly agitated by the volume of criticism over the colour. This puzzled him.

"Why," he asked, "do you keep repeating yourself?"

"Because … it's… red," said Mike, trying not to sound ungrateful for the tailor's efforts. Mike clearly found himself in an awkward position.

"This is true, but why do you keep repeating yourself?"

"It's not me," explained Mike, "it's my friend Wriggler. He repeats everything I say."

"No, I don't!"

"Well, you are at the moment."

"I'm not."

The otter's patience was beginning to wear a little threadbare. He placed the tail on the counter.

Mike pointed to the open pouch on his backpack. "This is Wriggler."

Wriggler stared warily at the otter. The otter gazed hungrily at Wriggler as if he had an overpowering desire to eat him. Wriggler shuddered and slid a little further inside the safety of the pouch.

"Am I to take it you won't be requiring the tail, or do you wish me to go ahead with the fitting?"

Mike remained quiet for a few moments before making his decision.

"If it's the only tail you've got, then I suppose I'll have to take it. I can't attend the summer fête without being properly dressed for the occasion."

"At last, we're getting somewhere," sighed Mr Stitch. "Bend over, so I can attach the tail."

Mike did as he was told. The tailor grabbed a passing Samson snail and slapped a dollop of extra strong glue upon Mike's behind. The tail was attached successfully.

All three stared into the full-length mirror at the appendage.

"It's a fine red tail," said Wriggler.

"It certainly is," agreed Mr Stitch.

"It definitely is a fine red tail. I must thank you for your assistance, Mr Stitch. It's just a shame it's not black."

The otter ignored Mike's last comment. He was in too much of a rush to shut the shop.

"If that's all, then I must be off. I have to visit the fête to buy some much-needed black thread."

Mike gathered up his backpack. Just as he was about to leave, he asked Mr Stitch if he'd care to join him and Wriggler on their way to Pembridge Town.

"We'll be taking the old towpath all the way there. You're more than welcome to join us"

The otter shook his head dismissively.

"Thank you for the offer, but I'll be going via the river. It's quicker and I can grab a snack along the way."

Mike fully understood.

"Once again, Mr Stitch, thank you for your help … and my grandad sends his regards."

Mike headed for the door and departed.

Outside the shop, Mike stood momentarily beneath the dark thicket of willow branches and peered above.

"I wonder where that strange voice came from!" he pondered.

Quite unexpectedly, a voice addressed him.

"I know, tell me about it."

It was the same booming voice as before and shook the ground Mike stood on.

Wriggler was so startled he shot down into the soil in the backpack pouch and buried himself from view.

Mike gazed around to see if he could see anyone. For some reason, he suspected the voice might not be as unfriendly as it sounded.

"You're looking very well today," said Mike, pretending he could see someone.

"I know, tell me about it," the voice answered back.

No matter which direction Mike looked, nothing unusual caught his eye.

"Have you been on holiday?" Mike enquired.

"About tell, I know me it," replied the voice, rather puzzlingly.

Mike still had no idea where the voice was coming from.

"This is all very odd," whispered Mike.

"It know, I tell about me," the voice replied.

Thereupon the shop door opened and out stepped

Mr Stitch, who happened upon Mike holding his head aloft.

"Don't worry about him," exclaimed the otter.

"Know I, tell it about me," said the voice.

Mike turned to face Mr Stitch, who was carrying a wicker basket full of fabric swatches and unwanted twine. Mr Stitch placed the basket on the floor and then attached a note to the door that read:

Tailor's Shop closed as I'm
attending the summer fête.
p.s. Free samples, please take.

Mike leaned over and removed some string from the basket. "It might come in useful on my travels," Mike thanked Mr Stitch, before placing the string in his backpack.

"If you were wondering about the voice, it belongs to Gantree, the weeping willow," explained the otter. "They're the only words he knows. He means no harm."

"About it, tell me I know," said Gantree.

Curiously, Gantree had stopped weeping and instead learned to talk, having memorized half a dozen words. To be precise, one sentence, which he used consistently and quite often in the wrong order.

How all this occurred is a story in itself. Over the

years, the chronicle has been embroidered upon and become punctuated with inaccuracies. In truth, Gantree woke up one morning and decided he was tired of being miserable and forever in tears. The only way he felt he could snap out of his weariness was to adopt a hobby.

By chance, a group of humans was passing by, talking and laughing. Gantree became fascinated by what he heard and decided he too wanted to converse, so he could enjoy life more and laugh instead of cry. He chose a sentence he overheard one of the humans using, which he liked the sound of, and remembered it. From that day onwards, Gantree would chatter through a knothole in his trunk to everyone who spoke beneath his branches.

However, because he was lazy, he never bothered to learn any more vocabulary. Instead, he decided just to jumble up the six words he already knew. As amusing as it may have sounded to him, it really was just gibberish.

"The words are grammatically correct and occasionally in the right order," explained Mr Stitch, "and as useful as these words are, they really are the only words Gantree has ever learned. I think of him more as a security guard. He wards off would-be burglars. It means I never need to lock my front door."

"About I, tell know me it," rumbled Gantree.

"You get used to him with time," assured Mr Stitch. "Although he can get a bit tedious."

Having heard the otter's explanation, Wriggler now felt more at ease and poked his head out of the pouch. There followed a short pause in the conversation, before all four answered in unison, "I know, tell me about it."

CHAPTER 6

A Very Peculiar Chant

Mike and Wriggler rejoined the trail of the mystery footprints on the abandoned towpath at Hollow Twine. Here, sections of the concrete path had cracked due to years of earth movement and harsh weather conditions, making it increasingly difficult for Mike to differentiate between the jumble of visible animal tracks. Spotting the occasional footprint confirmed he was heading in the right direction. That direction was Pembridge Town, where the summer fête was and where coincidently the path ended.

It was also along this part of the towpath that anglers occasionally fished for trout. On such days, Harvey would remain hidden from view, lying low on the riverbed.

Mike removed his skateboard from his backpack and put on his denim jacket. He then transferred Wriggler into the jacket's wide top pocket. From here on, Mike intended to skate to Pembridge Town. This was when Wriggler got to travel in style.

Wriggler loved nothing better than to feel the rush of cool air upon him as Mike gathered speed. They rounded a bend with ease, gliding up a slight incline before carving down the dip on the opposite side. As they approached a tight turn, Mike suddenly heard a weird chant floating on the breeze.

"Ooh, argh, eeh, ow
Ooh, argh, eeh, ow"

Mike swerved to handle the bend then made a sudden kick-stop, sending Wriggler almost flying. On the path ahead stood a triangular sign with the words PATH AHEAD CLOSED upon it. Mike and Wriggler stared at the sign.

"What now?" asked Wriggler as he fidgeted inside the pocket, trying to make himself comfortable again. "That chant sounds weird…"

"Ooh, argh, eeh, ow
Ooh, argh, eeh, ow"

"Stop fussing," said Mike, impatiently. "It's probably just … the rickety old watermill in the distance."

"I don't like the sound of it!" insisted Wriggler. "It's … weird." Wriggler always did look on the bleak side of things.

"Ooh, argh, eeh, ow
Ooh, argh, eeh, ow"

The mantra continued. Curiosity is the mother of sticky situations. Mike decided to investigate where the sound was coming from. The further forward he walked, the louder the chant became.

"Ooh, argh, eeh, ow
Ooh, argh, eeh, ow"

As they turned the bend, Mike stopped in his tracks.

Blocking the towpath ahead was a battalion of soldier ants, chanting. They stretched the width of the path and resembled a relay team. Each ant in the row was passing stones from one to the other. Surprisingly, the rocks looked way too heavy for one ant to carry. On the opposite side of the path, the stones were being arranged into a large pile.

Wriggler had never warmed to ants and always panicked at the sight of one. The vision of a whole battalion sent him into a fit. He shot out of sight inside the depths of the pocket.

"Ooh, argh, eeh, ow
Ooh, argh, eeh, ow"

Turn and turnabout, the chanting rhythm kept the production line operating smoother than a well-oiled engine.

Where the stones had originated from and where they were destined, and why they were being displaced seemed a lot of questions to ask, especially when the ants were so engrossed in their work.

Mike thought twice, and twice again, before crossing their path. He knew he had to get to the other side, but exactly how, he had yet to fathom out. Soldier ants are known to be unfriendly when disturbed. Their sting is as lethal as a bee sting. How he was to navigate them without disturbing them was another puzzle Mike had to figure out. Fortunately, they hadn't noticed him yet.

"Let's just go home," pleaded Wriggler as he poked his head back out of the pocket.

At the side of the path, Mike spotted a discarded wooden plank. It was resting vertically upon a mound just ahead of him. It didn't take long for Mike to devise a plan.

Mike whispered to Wriggler, "I'm going to make a jump for it."

"What?" questioned Wriggler. "I'd much rather we turn around and went back home?"

"Where's the fun in that!" chuckled Mike.

Wriggler was wholly unconvinced by the plan.

Mike walked back beyond the bend, clearing away any loose gravel or twigs that might get in his way. When he was ready, he placed his right hindfoot on the skateboard. Just as he was about to set off, a toad appeared and hopped aboard, introducing itself with a "croak!"

"Hey!" fired Mike as he leaned over and stroked it. "It's good luck to stroke a toad's skin."

"Rather you than me," quipped Wriggler, offhandedly.

At which point, the toad leaped off and continued on its merry way.

"Here goes." Mike pushed off along the path, gaining momentum. As he approached the bend, Wriggler ducked inside the pocket for fear of what was about to happen.

Mike hugged the bend, approached the vertical plank, and raced up towards the jump. Just before the drop, he ollied into the air gliding straight over the row of ants below.

Wriggler stuck his head out mid-flight to check

what was happening. "Argh!" he shrieked and promptly shot back inside the pocket.

As the skateboard descended, a rear wheel clipped the pile of stones, dislodging one, causing the stack to collapse. Mike landed unevenly, with a thud. The impact sent him veering into the tall grass verge where he toppled over, several yards ahead of the ants.

Stones careered across the path - the ants scattered in all directions, like dust in a breeze. Mike picked himself up and sped away faster than a hare escaping a poacher's bullet.

A short while later, along the towpath, when his breathing had become regular once more, Mike slowed down a little.

"That was close," gasped Mike, as he heaved a sigh of relief.

Wriggler had no words to summon up his feelings. Uncharacteristically, he remained quiet for the remainder of the journey, thankful to be in one piece.

On the outskirts of Pembridge Town, Mike rode past Vision Cottage, where the elderly humans Mr and Mrs Spottiswood resided. They'd lived in the cottage all their married years and knew most of the wildlife around them. During warm summer's evening's animals and insects would congregate on their rear lawn to gaze through the glass porch at the flickering vision box inside. Even nightbirds would watch from the twisted branches of the crab apple trees. Mrs Spottiswood always warmly welcomed all her guests into the garden. She occasionally left water and cookies on the porch steps for them to enjoy.

The vision box transmitted pictures on the local Bee Broadcasting Corporation network, the likes of which none of the animals, birds, or insects had ever seen before. The visions were often the topic for much debate and conversation the following day.

"Perhaps," Mike promised Wriggler, "if we have time on our way back this evening, I can stop off at the cottage to show you the vision box."

The Tail of 'Too Bad' Mike

CHAPTER 7

The Summer Fête

The summer fête took place in Pembridge Square, in the shadow of Hive Castle and the ominous Tower of the Winds. The Queen had given her consent for the afternoon to be a public holiday for all her subjects.

The square was decorated elaborately with bunting and large black and yellow banners depicting the Pembridge coat of arms - a hive and swarm of bees entwined around a large letter P positioned beneath a gold crown.

Mike and Wriggler arrived amid the hustle and bustle, the likes of which they had never experienced before. All manner of festivities, sideshows, and games were taking place. A hazelnut shy, a bat a rat stand (where the rat had craftily padded his backside), bin raffles, white elephant stalls, clowns, a flea ballet, tombola, performing circus animals, gypsy moth dancing, tug o' war, a stilt-walking crane fly, and row upon row of market stalls displaying merchandise and organic food. A medley of laughter and voices filled the air. What's more, today, by royal decree, the entertainment and grub were free.

Earthworms mixed with slugs, snails with insects. Squirrels, hares, field mice and grass snakes, scuttled around. A red fox, an otter, weasels, and badgers all took part in the games. Birds of numerous varieties, shrews and hedgehogs, took turns on the helter-skelter. Rabbits, butterflies, frogs, earwigs, and toads were eating loads and happily mixing together.

Weird entertainers performed tricks with sticks. A muddling grass snake that Wriggler thought brave, swallowed everything he was given, including a sword and a live pigeon, till the crowd roared their disapproval, and he let open his jaw and released the live bird on to the floor. A dragon-like lizard, the kind Mike and Wriggler had not encountered, blew gusts of fire higher and higher until the flames singed the feathers of a passing dove. After which he was promptly ordered to halt his act by an officer from the fire brigade under the Health and Safety Act. Never before had such a mixture of cultures been brought together so harmoniously beneath one sky.

As was the practice at public occasions, Queen Beetrice arrived upon her golden throne to observe all the activities and merriment. As usual, Lord and Lady Muck followed closely behind, making sure everybody adhered to the bowing rule. The Queen loved shopping and had a keen eye for a bargain; she missed nothing, and nothing passed her by. Indeed, she could glimpse a good deal a mile away and spent most of the afternoon stockpiling delicious snacks. For her, the event was a triumph in public relations, and for the Mucks, a brilliant coup to mask their mean and corrupt behaviour.

A contortionist field mouse dressed in a white elephant costume balanced cleverly on his trunk. A paddle of sitting ducks wearing colourful socks were mightily impressed with the mouse's prowess and applauded wildly. A gaggle of geese joined an audience of frogs in the open-air amphitheatre to gander at the Royal Ballet dancing *The Flame of Love*. When the fiery natured salamander turned into a prince, unlike the geese, the frogs didn't wince.

Sitting close by under the canopy of a gypsy tent, and dressed in a long shawl, was Madame Petronella, a clairvoyant tawny owl. Considered by some to be a foolish old windbag, others adhered to her every word. A small table with a translucent crystal ball upon it was placed in front of her. When she saw Mike approaching, she beckoned him over.

"Come, sit with me. I will give you a free reading," she offered.

Mike sat on the stool in front of the small table.

The argus-eyed owl gazed into the crystal ball. Slowly, she fell into a trance. Her jet-black pupils became dilated, and mist appeared inside the ball.

Wriggler was fascinated with the owl and the size of her enormous saucer eyes. For once in his life, he was not in the least bit anxious. He watched her every move with bated breath.

Madame Petronella removed her gaze from the crystal ball and directed it upon Mike. She exuded a sudden urgency as if to forewarn him of impending danger.

"I have two things to say but only one you must remember. Hindsight is a wonderful thing, so is intuition," advised the owl. "Take heed of the latter. Yours is strong. Use it wisely, let it guide you, and it will stand you in good stead."

The owl covered her crystal ball with her cloak to signify the reading was over.

Mike thanked the owl for her words of wisdom and promptly left. He felt peckish, so he made a beeline for the honey tasting stalls in front of the noisy Wall of Gabbling Gargoyles.

The Wall of Gabbling Gargoyles was centuries old and made of jagged flint rock. It defined one side of Pembridge Square. Each stone was shaped to resemble a gargoyle, and each head had a mouth that could talk the hind legs off a donkey. Their voluble tongues had got them into much trouble over the years.

Numerous insects and animals were sampling the various brands of honey from the pots displayed on the tables. Some were getting themselves into a right sticky mess. Mike joined in with the tasting.

There was honey for every occasion and every flavour you could wish for. There was even a deluxe pot of *Moon Honey* created especially for newlyweds.

Nearby, a group of weasels in white hats and white coats carrying clipboards were sampling the Summer Solstice honey, produced especially for the fête. Its secret properties were said to enhance significantly one's wellbeing if eaten regularly. The weasels were members of the judging committee and spoke with particularly brash voices. Each time they passed a critique, a Gabbling Gargoyle would mimic the sentence.

"It's a bit spicy, but spice is nice," repeated a Gabbling Gargoyle.

"I find it very sweet, and sweet is a treat," answered a smaller head.

"I find it quite sour like fennel flower," announced a spherical rock head.

"I think it's yuck, it tastes like muc…"

"You!" interrupted Lady Muck. "Give it here, you dawbake." She snatched the spoonful of honey from the weasel's paw. "It can't possibly be all those adjectives at once. What bunkum."

She swallowed a mouthful of honey. "Why … it is spicy, and spice is nice. Be done with your gabble, wall."

The weasels fell silent, as did the wall. Lady Muck slapped a winning rosette on the honey pot, then gathered up her skirt and strode off towards the balancing white mouse. "Don't dawdle," she snapped at her dithering husband in tow.

As soon as she was out of earshot, a gargoyle opened its mouth.

"Why … it is spicy, and spice is nice. Be done with your gabble, wall." Oh, and how the gargoyles howled with laughter.

Unbeknown to most of those attending the fête, the castle was also a hive of activity in preparation for that evening's Grand Banquet.

The banqueting hall stretched the entire length of the castle's ground floor. It was currently in the throes of being decorated in preparation for the occasion. Most of the nobility and gentry from the kingdom would be in attendance to celebrate the success of this year's fête, and it was imperative the room looked spick and span.

Mrs Washalot, the royal housekeeper, had taken it

upon herself to supervise the arrangements. Subsequently, she had spent a week of sleepless nights worrying about the details. She need not have vexed for her hard work, and thoroughness showed; the room looked spectacular.

The long banqueting table comfortably seated two hundred guests. It was dressed with crested china and magnificent floral displays of white and yellow honeysuckle, honewort, and bee balm that rivalled the blossoms on Turquoise Island.

As was the custom at such events, Queen Beetrice would be seated away from the prying eyes of her public at the far end of the table beneath the raised minstrel gallery. On either side of her would be her attendants, Lord and Lady Muck. For those not fortunate to be invited to the banquet, there would be a free party in the Square that evening at which everyone would be welcome.

Back in Pembridge Square, Mike was garnering much attention wherever he wandered.

"I see you came fitted-out for the occasion," remarked a passing grey squirrel.

Mike wondered what the squirrel was implying.

"Your tail, it's red!"

"Oh!" he suddenly remembered. "It's only temporary."

"I should hope so, too. If red tails became the fashion, what would us grey squirrels do?"

Just ahead, Mike noticed a group of female shrews crowded around a tall male shrew. The male shrew was commanding a lot of interest.

Mike's inquisitive mind got the better of him. He wandered over to take a closer look.

Handsome Cad had made a name for himself in Pembridge Town with his football skills and was delighting his female admirers with tales of his success on the pitch. Clad in the latest fashionable sportswear, he cut a dashing figure. It wasn't until the footballer turned to demonstrate his back heel kick that Mike saw the evidence he'd been pursuing … the shrew had two tails attached to his rear. Mike recognised one of the tails as his and realised this had to be the shrew Harvey had told him about.

Mike pushed his way to the front of the crowd. Wriggler sensed trouble and ducked for cover inside the pocket, leaving only his head poking out. Mike confronted Cad.

"How come you have two tails when I don't have one?"

The crowd went quiet. Cad was not one to be made a fool of, especially in front of so many beautiful females. He swung his two tails in defiance.

"And who are you?" asked Cad mockingly. "Why,

if I'm not mistaken, you do have a tail ... and it's RED!" he laughed.

All the female shrews laughed in accord with the conniving Cad. Mike stood his ground.

"My name is Mike, and my tail is false ... I had it made especially for the fête."

"I'll vouch for that," announced Mr Stitch, who had just that moment arrived on the scene. "I made it this very day."

The crowd mumbled their astonishment.

"I believe your second tail belongs to me and I can prove it," claimed Mike. "Allow me to demonstrate."

A female shrew named Penny was so shocked by Mike's claim, she lowered her head in shame. Penny had a big crush on Cad, and, in her eyes, he could do no wrong.

"I don't believe a word of it," she wailed, then promptly fainted on the spot.

The penny had dropped. Mike's intuition was working overtime. He had no intention of backing down.

Queen Beetrice was browsing nearby and became curious to know what all the excitement was about. She ordered her guards to carry her throne over, so she could take a look. Lord and Lady Muck followed dutifully behind.

By now, a sizeable crowd had assembled, some

innocently thinking it was a sideshow.

"It's the tug o' war," called out one onlooker, as the gathering crowd grew larger.

Dodger, the rat, a ticket tout, was not one to miss out on money-making schemes and promptly took bets on who would win the bout.

Cad had no intention of being made to look a clown. He stood his ground.

"Just because I have the perfect physique, you're jealous. Do you really expect anyone to believe the twaddle you speak? If you think my second tail is yours, prove it."

Dodger, the rat, was having none of that and saw a devious angle to increase his odds. He promptly addressed the crowd.

"Listen up! If it's fashionable to wear two tails, I'll eat my hat. How come I don't have two and I'm the king rat?"

The crowd was fifty-fifty in agreement, and a flourish of bets came flooding in.

The atmosphere was tense. Mike took up his defence.

"I'll ask you once more, and only once. Give me back my tail, and I'll walk away. Otherwise, I'll take it by force."

The excitement among the crowd intensified.

"Now, what have we here?" enquired Wing

Commander Hari Ha-ha as he buzzed in overhead.

"It's 'too bad' Mike," called out a grass snake that had clearly sided with Cad. "Just 'cause he's got a miserable red tail, he's now after one of Cad's."

"A MISERABLE red tail?" protested Mr Stitch. "I'll have you know, it's poppy-coloured and made from a skein of the finest twisted silk thread in the kingdom!"

The Wing Commander looked highly concerned about the situation and made an emergency landing on top of a spectator's hat.

Lord Muck pushed his way to the front of the crowd.

"How entertaining, a tug o' war. I'll be the judicator. Whoever is first to pull the other one by their tail across the line is the winner." Lord Muck marked a line in the dust with his walking cane. "Any foul play, and the culprit goes straight to the Tower." Some spectators cowered with fear as soon as they heard the Tower mentioned. "Take up your positions and commence tugging after four."

Cad had a venomous tongue on him and was spoiling for a fight.

"Finders, keepers, losers, weepers," called out Cad, in a rabble-rousing effort to muster more support from the crowd, then flicked not one, but two tails to impress all the attractive young females.

Mike squared up to Cad and awaited the count.

"Oh! No," yelped Wriggler, as he shot out of sight. "Can't we just go home?"

"After four," announced Lord Muck. "Four ... three ... two ... one. Let the game commence."

A cheer rang out from the crowd as Cad feverishly lashed out at Mike, who ducked to avoid his aim. Mike lost his balance and fell over but quickly regained his stand, then leaped on Cad and pushed him to the ground. In the scuffle that followed, Cad grabbed Mike's red tail and, with a furious tug, yanked it off, much to the horror of those spectators with a weak disposition.

Before Cad had time to consider, Mike retaliated and lunged for one of Cad's tails.

"That's my tail you've stolen, and I want it back!"

With titanic strength, Mike pulled and pulled until finally, the tail detached itself. The force sent Mike tumbling backward, where he fell to the ground hitting his head with a thud, right in front of the Queen's throne. He lay there, stunned and motionless.

Such shameful behaviour the Queen had never encountered before and was flabbergasted.

"You thieving shrew," claimed Cad, as he pointed a claw of blame at Mike.

"What is that shrew's name?" demanded Queen

Beetrice.

"'Too Bad' Mike," called out a bystander.

As ever, the Queen's first Lady of the Bedchamber couldn't wait to put her two penn'orth in.

"Why even his name has BAD in it," declared Lady Muck.

"Who would have thought it? A false tail! It looked so legit," remarked a passing slug violinist who was running late for a performance in the orchestra pit at the amphitheatre. "Too bad Mike about losing your tail … a shrew without a tail is like … a shell without a snail."

"You are what you are… but you aren't always what you say you are," spoke Madam Petronella in defence of Mike's actions.

"Off with his head," called out another spectator.

"And just who's head should that be?" asked an inquisitive hiccupping duck while in the throes of knitting a black and red woollen sock. She clearly felt the axe should fall elsewhere - perhaps implying on the neck of a bureaucrat!

"How exciting this is. Let's have a trial to determine the outcome," commanded Queen Beetrice. "We haven't had a trial in ages."

"Arrest him at once," ordered Lord Muck," and take him to the Tower to await trial."

"Arrest, who, and what for?" enquired a guard.

"Why, 'Too Bad' Mike, you blithering fool," insisted Lord Muck, "for theft!"

Before Mike knew what was happening, the guards had surrounded him, and he was carried off to the ominous Tower of the Winds.

"And bring that tail with you," demanded Lord Muck. "We'll need it as evidence."

"Which one?" asked a guard, sounding confused.

Lord Muck hesitated for a few moments before answering. "Why … both of them, you hare-brained idiot."

The guard picked up the two tails and carried them away.

"I'll see you all in court at five o'clock, sharp … and don't be late," announced Lord Muck to the assembled crowd. "I have a banquet to attend this evening that I do not intend to miss."

"Gosh!" swallowed the clairvoyant owl, as she let out a yowl. "I must get help, I must get help."

Mike disappeared into the distance as the guards carried him away to the Tower of the Winds to await trial at the Court of Salazar.

"I never knew a quiet day. Of this, I must confess. Whenever I go out with Mike, we end up in a mess," muttered Wriggler from inside the pocket he was hiding.

Meanwhile, back in Pembridge Square, Handsome Cad had time to burn, time to lick his wounded pride, and time to concoct false evidence that he could present in court in his favour.

The Queen was most excited at the prospect of a trial. As were Lord and Lady Muck. It would round the afternoon off nicely.

"There's nothing like a gripping trial to work up an appetite," enthused Lady Muck to Her Majesty.

"I agree," concurred the Queen while nibbling on a chocolate whirl. "Anything that works up an appetite, I greatly encourage." She then bit into the chocolate and sunk her long tongue deep inside the soft vanilla filling, scooping out a large dollop. A look of bliss lit up her face.

"You know, I really ought to stop off at the Chocolate Shop," the Queen decided, "to purchase a few essentials."

"By all means, ma'am… we still have a whole hour to enjoy before the trial commences."

The Queen sank back into the plump cushions she was reclining on and nibbled further into her chocolate whirl.

The Avenue of Pembridge cut through Pembridge

Square from east to west and was the town's main thoroughfare. It was, in fact, a man-made path that had long since fallen into disrepair. To all the animals, insects, and birds, it was the town centre, where all the main buildings stood and where everything happened.

On the northeast corner of the avenue was a wooden drawbridge known locally as the Widow's Walk that led to the arched entrance of the Tower of the Winds. The drawbridge acquired its sinister name because it widowed the wife of any prisoner interned within. Once a prisoner was locked inside, there was no means of escape.

Just as the royal procession arrived at the northeast corner of the square, the drawbridge was lowered to take possession of its latest occupant, 'Too Bad' Mike.

Sitting on the stone steps beside the drawbridge was the old hiccupping duck. She wore a platitude of weariness upon her face, formed from months of waiting for her husband, Dr Quack, the former local practitioner. He was also imprisoned in the Tower. Here, she would sit every day for an hour, knitting socks for the poor. She developed hiccups a year ago after receiving the devastating news that her beloved husband had been charged with treason and banished to the Tower. Though she had tried every cure for hiccups known to birds, she had not been able to rid herself of the affliction. In solidarity with her husband, she had vowed to sit on the stone steps daily in the hope he might catch a glimpse of her from his cell window in the Tower.

As the royal procession passed by, Lady Muck tossed a disapproving glance at the old hiccupping duck.

"And what pray is that duck clucking on about?" demanded Lady Muck, sternly, to one of the accompanying Royal Guards.

"She has hiccups, My Lady," replied the guard, as the duck let forth another guttural burp.

"Hiccups are like a dribbling nose … hugely irritating. Tell the duck to put a sock in it at once," Lady Muck instructed the guard. "That's an order."

With that said, the royal entourage passed by, on towards the much frequented Chocolate Shop.

As regards the hiccupping duck, Lady Muck's reproach was water off her back. The duck carried on regardless, knitting her woollen sock.

The Tail of 'Too Bad' Mike

CHAPTER 8

Awake! Awake!

Just as the royal procession arrived outside the Chocolate Shop; and just as the hiccupping duck knitted the last stitch to complete her sock; just as the violinist slug struck his first note in the orchestra pit at the outdoor amphitheatre; and just as the Royal Guard delivered the two tails to the Court of Salazar; Madame Petronella landed at the nest of the slowest Carrier pigeon in the whole of the kingdom's aviation history.

Just as Handsome Cad came up with a convincing alibi; and just as Dodger the rat finished counting all his takings from his illegal betting scam; just as Mr Stitch bought the finest black cotton thread from the market stall; and just as Wing Commander Hari Ha-ha assembled a squadron of the bravest RAF fighter pilots he could gather; Madame Petronella let forth a piercing hoot.

"Awake! Awake!"

The tawny owl shrieked into the pigeon's ear.

"Awake! Awake!"

The plump pigeon slowly stirred from a deep slumber. Known for being absent-minded and a little stubborn, this particular pigeon had recently retired from homing duties and was now a part-time postie, delivering for the Pigeon Post.

"I must get news to Portobello Creek of a great injustice that has been done. How long will it take you to deliver it?" asked Petronella with urgency in her voice.

The pigeon's expression changed from concern to a look of thoughtfulness before resting into a gaze of optimism. During this drawn-out process of consideration, the owl seriously wondered whether she'd get more response from a wooden stool pigeon. Finally, the pigeon thrust its right wing outward into the moving airstream to check the wind velocity before folding it neatly back by its side.

"I could be there just before five o'clock... that's if the wind blows me in the right direction."

Petronella knew Mike's trial at the Court of Salazar commenced at five, and as far as she could detect, there really wasn't much wind about today.

"Could you not get there sooner?" she asked, impatiently. "The trial commences at five, and I need to get a witness there to attend."

The pigeon shook his head, unsure what to say.

"I could try and speed things up a little, just as long as you don't weigh me down with too much information and too many words to deliver," suggested the pigeon.

"How about if I was to tell you to deliver this and only this," replied Petronella, anxiously.

"And what might that be?" enquired the pigeon.

"This...," said the owl, rather hastily. Her patience was beginning to wear thin.

"What ... just 'THIS'?" interrupted the pigeon.

"No, not just 'THIS,'" screeched the owl, in exasperation. "You keep interrupting me before I finish the sentence."

"Do I? Well, I'm sorry about that, but I'm getting a bit confused about what words you want me to deliver."

The clairvoyant owl inhaled a deep, soothing breath of fresh air before continuing.

"I'll ask you calmly because I'm a calm owl that believes greatly in good karma and passing it on," Madame Petronella informed the pigeon, who looked even more bewildered than at the start of the conversation. "Mike, the shrew, has lost his tail and believes Handsome Cad has stolen it. While trying to apprehend Cad at the summer fête, Mike was arrested under the orders of Lord Muck and is at this very moment imprisoned in the Tower of the Winds awaiting trial."

The pigeon could barely believe what he was hearing and bolted upright with astonishment.

"His trial commences at five o'clock. If we don't help him, he could end up being imprisoned for life."

The pigeon gulped in dread at the thought of such a thing.

"I need you to deliver a message to Mike's Grandfather Gus, who lives on the old houseboat at Portobello Creek. This is the message ... listen carefully." Petronella spoke with calm authority. "Urgent assistance required at the Court of Salazar. Mike is in serious trouble," she inhaled slowly. "There ends the message."

The pigeon looked even more alarmed than he had done before.

"That's thirteen words if I've counted correctly. Will you require a reply?" the pigeon asked eagerly.

"Not necessarily," replied Madame Petronella. "Actions speak louder than words if you get my drift."

"I come from good stock. My great-great-great-great uncle worked on secret reconnaissance missions in World War II and carried messages back and forth from the front line. He is one of only thirty-two pigeons to have been awarded the Dickin Medal for bravery."

"Impressive," said Madame Petronella, whose patience was slowly eroding away. "Let's hope such valour still runs in the family."

The Carrier pigeon had to think twice about that but failed to reply. Instead, he poked his beak into his pigeonhole to find a telegram card but could not find one.

"I'm all out of telegram cards," the pigeon informed Petronella.

The owl blinked in disbelief. "Perhaps, if you were just to remember the message, it would suffice."

"My memory is not what it was when I was a youngster, but I'll keep repeating the message out loud so as not to forget it while I'm flying. It'll give me something to think about during the journey," declared the pigeon.

"If you must, by all means, do but be very careful not to let this information fall behind enemy lines," warned the owl.

"I see…," said the pigeon cautiously.

The pigeon went quiet for a moment as he worked out the quickest route to fly to Portobello Creek.

"I'll follow the river … that way, I won't get distracted, and I could knock thirty-minutes off the journey," decided the pigeon.

"As you wish," Madame Petronella agreed.

"A shrew without a tail is like … a postie without mail," chuckled the pigeon, as he slipped his postbag over his shoulder. He then opened his wings, leaped out of his nest, and rose up into the air with all the ferocity and strength he could muster.

"Speed be with you," called out Madame Petronella. "Speed be with you."

Due to the pigeon's habit of reciting out loud any messages he had to deliver, news of Mike's plight spread rapidly. Along the River Brae's riparian banks, all the animals, insects, and birds, from sleepy Willow Twine, past Turquoise Island and Pembridge Creek, heard the news. Finally, the pigeon arrived at Portobello Creek and swooped down to the houseboat, where he landed with a pronounced bounce on the canvas canopy overhanging Grandfather Gus's hammock.

"Awake! Awake!" cooed the pigeon, loudly. "Awake! Awake!"

Grandfather Gus bolted upright in the hammock and rubbed his bleary eyes. "What on earth was that?" he called out.

The pigeon poked his head down under the fringed edge of the canopy, giving Grandfather Gus quite a shock.

"And where, might I ask, did you come from?" Grandfather Gus sounded rather annoyed at being disturbed.

"Well, originally, I'm from northern Scotland. I was born on a small inhospitable island way up near the Shetlands. Truth is, I'm glad I migrated ... that place did my head in..."

"No, No," interrupted Grandfather Gus, who was beginning to wish he'd never asked. "I meant, where have you just come from?"

"Oh! Well, why didn't you say that in the first place?" asked the pigeon, sounding somewhat confused.

"I thought I did ... but, hey ho, maybe I should have said it less as a rhetorical question and more as a statement of surprise." Grandfather Gus really had lost the Carrier pigeon at this point.

The pigeon's cheeks slowly began to blush bright red.

"You'd better fly down here," advised Grandfather Gus, "before you turn into a robin."

The pigeon had no idea what Grandfather Gus was implying but took his advice and swooped down and landed on the hammock below.

"I have an important telegram to deliver. So important, you must memorise it then swallow it immediately," spoke the pigeon with great seriousness.

Due to the subject matter and sensitivity the news warranted, the Carrier pigeon decided to relay an unabridged, overly-embroidered version of the story. Needless to say, the recount was told with as much tact as would have been used by one of the heads on the Wall of Gabbling Gargoyles.

Grandfather Gus sighed as he waited patiently for the pigeon to cut to the chase. Finally, with all the facts laid out before him like jumbled pieces of a jigsaw, Grandfather Gus methodically pieced one and one together to get to the truth.

At that moment, Harvey, the trout, leaped out of the water as if he were attempting to jump through a hoop. He looked so distraught over the news of Mike's imprisonment he could barely string two syllables together for fear of blurting out his anger. He then swam back underwater.

For sure, it was time to act. A plan must be conceived, a plan of wise and significant action.

Grandfather Gus clambered down the rope ladder on to a raft moored alongside the houseboat. The raft was buoyant and had a single mast at the fore with a blue canvas sail attached. It was the handiwork of Grandfather Gus, who believed it to be unsinkable.

Indeed, so steadfast was his belief, he'd christened it *Titanic*, to suggest great strength. At a push, it carried four crew. It was constructed from various bits and pieces he'd retrieved from the riverside, including an oblong biscuit tin and driftwood lashed together with vines and hardy grasses. Perched on the mast's crown was a real crow's nest, which he'd found abandoned in the coppice.

Grandfather Gus unfurled the sail, then tied a loop with a bowline knot on a length of string and secured the opposite end to a metal ring at the fore of the raft.

On cue, Harvey, the trout, poked his head out of the river to see what was going on.

"Glide into the loop on the end of the string," Grandfather Gus instructed Harvey, as he hurled the length into the water.

Harvey followed the instructions and slid his body into the loop. It fitted his waist perfectly like a belt.

"Fly onboard," Grandfather Gus summoned the Carrier pigeon, who was watching from the deck of the houseboat with eyes wider than saucers. "You can be my lookout."

The pigeon could think of nothing more thrilling and swooped down into the crow's nest on the mast, causing the vessel to move unevenly, sending Grandfather Gus almost teetering overboard.

Gus grabbed the mast to steady himself, then called

out to Harvey, "to Pembridge Town. We have a trial to attend in court."

Harvey slipped into first gear, and the raft floated off with the breeze in its sail.

Along the riverbanks, from Portobello Creek to Westbourne Creek, past Turquoise Island to Willow Twine and beyond, animals, birds, and insects lined the route to cheer Grandfather Gus and Harvey on their way.

"To the Tower, we will head, in the court we will fight, to save Mike is our pledge," became the rallying call as the raft sailed ever closer to Pembridge.

All the animals, birds, and insects became so caught up in the excitement, they followed along the riverside to show their support for Grandfather Gus in his quest to get his grandson released.

Meanwhile, back in Pembridge Square, Mr Stitch happened to catch sight of Wing Commander Hari Ha-ha, who seemed in a fearsome rush to get somewhere. "Wing Commander," called out Mr Stitch, in a bid to grab his attention.

The Wing Commander stopped in mid-air and turned to see who had called his name.

"Mr Stitch," buzzed the Wing Commander, looking

quite flustered. "You might just be the person I need to talk to."

The Wing Commander flew down beside the otter and proceeded to tell Mr Stitch how he'd devised a plan to help Mike escape from the Tower of the Winds. Mr Stitch was so excited to hear the news, he promptly offered to help.

"I have some information that may be beneficial for you to know," revealed Mr Stitch. He promptly relayed details of Mike's visit to his shop that morning. "I believe Mike left the shop with something that could be jolly useful to aid his escape." Lest he was overheard, the otter imparted this interesting datum under his breath.

CHAPTER 9

Tower of the Winds

The Tower of the Winds overlooked the east wall of Hive Castle. In the afternoon sun, the jail cast a long shadow over the northeast corner of Pembridge Square. Lord Muck ordered its construction. It was a constant reminder to the locals of the dastardly deeds the Mucks had administered under their authority and the powerful grip they wielded over Queen Beetrice.

The structure was, in fact, the hollow trunk of a dead beech tree with the prison built inside. Its design was based upon the ancient Tower of the same name in Athens, erected to honour the eight winds. The Tower in Pembridge had only one usable floor located at the top of the trunk with eight chambers, and eight shuttered windows but only seven doors. A central spiral staircase led directly into an anti-chamber. Inside this chamber was a sealed window. A heavy wooden door led to the seven separate cells. All the cells apart from the furthest had two doors and a window and were interconnecting.

As warder of the Tower, Dawlok, the dormouse, held the principal position of turnkey. Powerfully muscled, he wore a black leather mask that cleverly revealed only his eyes, nose, and mouth. Dawlok was the protector of the Tower and the guardian of its prisoners. For his services, he received free food and lodgings. Legend had it, no one who entered the jail had ever escaped past Dawlok.

Each of the seven cells faced a point on the compass and was named after one of the eight wind deities that blew in that direction - Kaikias, Apeliotes, Eurus, Notus, Livas, Zephyrus, and Skiron. Boreas, the north wind, was the locum tenens should any of the other winds be taken ill or go on vacation.

The lock on each cell door was positioned on the exterior to prevent the occupant from picking the lock to escape. However, as the adjacent cell door was inside six of the cells, the prisoner could attempt to pick that lock. If successful, however, it would only gain him entry into the adjacent cell. The furthest chamber in the circle had only one door and a window. This cell housed any life prisoners, who would be shackled to the wall, making absconding doubly tricky. The only feasible escape route without detection from Dawlok was through a window. There was one drawback to this. As soon as the shuttered window was opened, a ferocious gale would blow into the cell, pinning its occupant against the wall, thereby rendering him immobile. The window could only be shut if and when the wind ceased.

After taking custody of his latest captive, Dawlok dragged Mike through three cells before reaching the only empty chamber available, Notus, named after the south wind.

Dawlok unlocked the door and thrust Mike onto the cell floor. "A shrew without a tail is like ... a warder without a jail," cackled the jailer, mercilessly. "The Royal Guard will be back in an hour to escort you to court."

Dawlok slammed the door shut and turned the heavy key twice to lock it.

Mike lay on the cold, dank floor for a few minutes, gathering his wits. He gently massaged the bump on the back of his head while allowing his eyes to wander inquisitively around the room. The only features he could distinguish were the two wooden doors and the low rectangular shuttered window that cast shards of light onto the floor.

He rose carefully on all fours and steadied himself before crossing over to one of the doors. The door had no handle and was locked. He then moved over to the shuttered window and stretched up to peer through a crack. Years of grime and cobwebs made it difficult to see anything. He tried wiping a small section with his paw and managed to see outside. Laid out many feet below was the bustling fête in Pembridge Square.

It soon dawned on Mike he was inside the Tower of the Winds and figured the cell must be facing south, for, in the distance, he could distinguish the course of the River Brae.

Mike loosened the straps on his backpack and let it fall to the floor. Only then did he remember Wriggler and hurriedly checked inside his denim jacket pocket. Wriggler wasn't there. Only the soil remained. Mike then checked the pouch on his backpack; that too was empty.

No matter how many times Mike went over everything, he just couldn't figure out where Wriggler might be. "Perhaps he'd fallen out of his pocket during the fight in Pembridge Square," wondered Mike. The thought made his stomach churn. If he'd lost Wriggler, he knew the chances of ever seeing him again were slim. The more he dwelt upon it, the more he believed his friend had come to some harm, and the more he felt wholly responsible. A great wash of sadness came upon him, unlike any he had ever experienced before. He lurched backward against the wall and slid listlessly to the floor, where he lowered his head into his paws.

"You didn't look very far," spoke a shrill voice from above.

Mike lifted his head and gazed around the cell to see where the voice came from. He couldn't see a soul and wondered if his mind was playing tricks.

"I said ... you didn't look very far," restated the voice, in a weird, kind of upside-down, squeal. "He's on the straw bed in the corner."

Mike hadn't even noticed the straw. He stood up and squinted his eyes to see which corner the voice meant.

"The one beside you ... just along from the window," directed the voice.

Mike turned to his left and saw the straw on the floor.

"Summer fête! ... more like a fated summer," came the familiar tones of Wriggler. "I got bored waiting for you to stir, so I went for a wander to check out the accommodation. Not exactly the Ritz, is it?"

Mike knelt down beside the bed of straw. Wriggler had a smug expression upon his face.

"Crying, were you?" asked Wriggler.

"No ... not at all," muttered Mike, embarrassed by the mere suggestion. "I ... err," coughed Mike, awkwardly, "had some dust in my eye."

"I could do with some water," requested Wriggler. "I'm a bit dehydrated." Mike reached into his backpack and removed the dandelion and burdock bottle. "After I've had a drink, you can lift me back into your pocket. It's a bit nippy out here."

Mike did exactly as he was told and lifted Wriggler back into his jacket pocket.

"A right mess you've got us into," pointed out Wriggler while surveying the cell. "Unless you've got a door key, it looks like our only means of escape is through the window."

"It's a big drop," announced Mike, slightly disheartened.

"I don't suppose you've brought a parachute with you?" enquired the voice from above.

Mike and Wriggler looked at one another with puzzled expressions.

"I'm up here in the battery," called down the mysterious voice.

Mike and Wriggler raised their heads and saw a bat's head poking through a hole in the ceiling.

"I'll rephrase that," decided the bat. "It used to be the battery. It's now abandoned apart from me. All the other bats got fed up hanging around this hellish place and flew off when some idiot wind blew a hole in the roof."

"Strange," mumbled Wriggler to Mike.

The dark-brown bat flew out of the hole and landed upside down on a ceiling rafter below.

"I've been watching you two for a while," continued the bat.

"The battery," queried Mike, "is it up in the roof?"

"Yes," answered the bat. "In the loft ... as is the hole."

"So, how come you haven't flown away?" asked Mike inquisitively.

"Truth be known, I'm a bit of a loner ... I prefer being on my own unless I have visitors," admitted the bat. "Anyway, who are you, and what are you in here for?"

"I'm Mike," said Mike, "and I'm Wriggler."

Mike continued, "all I know is Handsome Cad stole my tail, and when I tried to get it back from him, I ended up bumping my head, and now I'm in here."

"That's some story," remarked the bat.

"Well, it's true," piped up Wriggler, who, for some reason - though he couldn't quite work out why - rather liked the bat. "I know 'cause I was there."

"Anyway," asked Mike, "how come you can see when everybody knows bats are blind?"

The bat did not bat an eyelid.

"The saying 'blind as a bat' is a pure myth spread by humans!" affirmed the bat. "Although we use echolocation to navigate, we also have some vision, albeit only black and white ... which can be extremely useful in the dark."

"I can imagine," agreed Wriggler, who was forever bumping his head in the dark labyrinth of tunnels he resided in on Turquoise Island.

"And what sort of bat are you?" asked Wriggler, with great interest.

"A common Pipistrelle," replied the bat, matter-of-factly.

"That's an unusual name," commented Wriggler, as he attempted miserably to pronounce it.

"As we're trunked up here in the same cell, how about if we were to call you Pip for short?" proposed Mike, in a show of neighbourliness.

"As you wish," shrugged the bat. "Pip, it is!"

"Who's in the cell next door?" asked Mike, changing the subject all of a sudden.

"I don't know," stated Pip. "Why don't you take a look through the keyhole?"

Mike picked up his backpack and placed it against the door. He then clambered up the bag and peered through the keyhole. The next-door chamber looked equally as dismal and uninviting as the one he was locked in. Lying on the straw bed was an elderly drake that appeared to be shackled to the wall. The duck wore a pair of brown knee-high woollen socks covered in bright yellow spots. A manacle was attached to his left ankle.

Mike called to the jailbird through the keyhole.

"Hello."

The drake stirred from his bed as he tried to determine where the voice was coming from.

"Over here, by the door," Mike called out.

The drake stood and waddled over to the door; his metal chain just managing to reach. He peered through the keyhole.

"I'm Mike ... the new kid on the block."

"Hello, Mike ... I saw you being hauled in. You looked in a pretty bad shape," disclosed the duck.

"It was nothing, really ... just a bump to my head," said Mike, dismissively.

"Sore, is it?" asked the drake, as if he knew a thing or two about bumps. "I only ask because I'm a doctor. Dr Quack's my name."

"No, I'm okay. I'll be fine ... Listen, I need to escape. Is there any other way out of here except through the window?" implored Mike.

Dr Quack went quiet for a moment as if he was racking his brain. "I've been in here for a year without any trial. If there was an escape route, I'd know about it by now. The only way I can see me getting out of here is in a coffin … over Widow's Walk," professed the duck, gloomily.

"What were you imprisoned for?" enquired Mike.

"Treason … I looked at the Queen while I was examining a troublesome wart on her face," confessed the doctor.

"Hmmm," mumbled Mike, "not a pretty sight."

Mike watched as the duck slowly moved away from the door and waddled back to his straw bed.

"Don't worry, Dr Quack," Mike called out. "I'll come up with something, I promise … I'll get us out."

Mike jumped down from the backpack and crossed over to the window. For the next few minutes, he paced back and forth across the cell in deep thought, rocking Wriggler almost asleep. Finally, he came to a standstill directly in front of the window. Once more, he peered through the crack in the shutter at Pembridge Square below and the River Brae's distinctive curves in the distance.

"I'm going to open the window shutter. It's our only means of escape."

A deep frown formed along Wriggler's brow.

"If you do," responded Pip, "the wind will blow a gale."

"But it can't blow forever," insisted Mike.

"Well, I'm not sticking around to see," interrupted

the bat. "You'll find me up in the battery. Wake me when it's over."

Pip promptly disappeared through the hole in the ceiling.

Mike opened his backpack, took out his skateboard, then strapped the bag on his back. "Keep your head down, Wriggler. I'm opening the shutter. I'll get us out of here if it's the last thing I do."

"Oh! No," wailed Wriggler, as he plunged into the depths of the pocket.

Mike steadied himself. "Here goes..." He lifted the latch and ducked, pulling the skateboard close to his body for protection.

The shutters burst open in a raging temper, and a violent gust of wind entered the cell, howling like a wild cat. Such was its force, it lifted the straw bed and hurled it around the room. The squally wind blew relentlessly at such a rate, it chilled everything in sight with its icy breath.

Perhaps it wasn't the smartest idea Mike had ever had, but his intuition told him otherwise. Neither did he have a rope to scale down the side of the Tower. Without one, how did he expect to escape? Quite what Mike expected to happen next, he had yet to fathom out. All he could do for the moment was to hold his back firmly against the wall and cling on to his skateboard for dear life, and hope the wind would subside.

"It has to die down at some point," Mike kept pleading. "It has to."

Yet, the wind blew stronger and stronger, showing no signs of diminishing in strength.

After a gale comes a period of calm - as the mighty wind doth blow, at some point, the wind will lose its velocity. That moment arrived. The wind got winded and gradually decreased until finally, it stopped blowing altogether. The room fell eerily silent and tranquil once more.

Mike inhaled a deep breath as if to embrace the calmness. The rush of excitement had left him feeling incredibly hungry.

"I knew I should have eaten a second breakfast this morning," he mumbled to himself.

"I beg your pardon?" came a deep booming voice from outside.

Mike froze and remained silent.

"I beg your pardon?" the voice repeated. "I didn't quite catch what you just said."

Mike slowly raised his body and turned towards the window. As he did, he came face to face with a gigantic, bearded head, the largest he'd ever seen. Floating in the air was the mythical, amber-winged apparition Boreas, the north wind, dressed in a long flowing cloak and short pleated tunic. In one hand, he held a twisted conch shell.

The figure smiled affably.

"Sorry, but I didn't catch what you said. One of my ears is playing up. I really must get it syringed."

The ghostly figure was quite intimidating.

Mike mustered up all the courage he could and replied, in what emerged to be the highest tone in his vocal range. "I knew I should have eaten a second breakfast this morning," he repeated, squeakily.

"Yes, I fully agree. One should always start the day with a hearty breakfast ... two sounds even better. I must remember that tomorrow morning before I set out for work," replied the figure as he unruffled his cloak among the swirling undercurrents in the air. "Sorry, I forgot to introduce myself. I'm Boreas ... the north wind."

"How strange," thought Mike, who was positive the cell was facing south.

"I'm Mike."

"Very pleased to be acquainted with you, Mike," motioned Boreas, as his hand reached in through the window.

Boreas momentarily laughed, then quickly retracted his arm.

"Sorry, I forgot ... you can't shake my hand because

I'm a ghostly wind. Never mind, we can still be friends," Boreas assured Mike.

Boreas could blow a fierce gale when he wanted. The other wind deities referred to him as the weatherman, for he had the extraordinary power to accurately predict the weather. Though it is undoubtedly true that winds do have certain divine powers, they also bring torrential rain, bountiful harvests, and devilish storms. However, no other wind held the uncanny precision of prediction that Boreas possessed.

"So, why are you locked up in here, young Mike?" asked Boreas, while straightening the ruffles in his long, flowing cloak.

"To be honest, I'm not sure," declared Mike. "All I know is, some cad stole my tail, and when I tried to get it back, I ended up bumping my head. Now I'm in here."

"That is a sorry story," remarked Boreas as he stroked his pointed chin.

"It's true," stressed Wriggler, who had just poked his head up out of Mike's top pocket to take a look at Boreas. "I was there."

"I see," said the friendly wind. "And just who might you be?"

"Wriggler … from Turquoise Island."

"Excuse me for asking," piped up Mike, "but, how

come you're the north wind, yet this cell faces south?"

"Notus is blowing a sickie ... laryngitis, or something similar, so I blew in to cover for him," announced Boreas, rather wearily. "I appear to be in full-time employment at the moment, and I'm feeling quite exhausted. I really can't remember the last time I had a day off."

Boreas opened his mouth and attempted to blow, but nothing came out. "You see, I'm all blown out."

Mike hollered up to the battery. "You can come out now, Pip. The coast is clear."

Mike, Wriggler, and Boreas all stared up at the ceiling as the bat poked her head through the hole.

"I apologize for the gale," expressed Boreas, "sometimes, I just have to get it off my chest, so to speak."

"As you must," affirmed the bat, as she flew down onto the rafter below. "I've got used to the odd gust or two. It comes with the territory."

"It really is too bad Mike to hear you've lost your tail," proclaimed Boreas. "Why a shrew without a tail is like ... a storm without a gale," he laughed to himself. "I must assist you in finding it at once."

"Can you predict the weather, Boreas?" interrupted Wriggler. "If so, you're just the person I need to talk to about the latest progress on the weather front. I have a feeling there's a drought on the way."

"Well … let me see," said Boreas, as he lifted his arm up into the sky. "The hot weather will continue for most of the forthcoming week, but if you need a downpour, I'm sure I could arrange it."

Wriggler was beside himself with joy.

"A shower, or two, would be more than enough to top up the river," confirmed Wriggler, gratefully.

"Then, leave it with me. I'll see what I can do."

"Look…," Mike called out, as he pointed up into the sky. "Over there!"

Away in the distance but not too far away, a swarm of bees was gathering. Mike, Wriggler, Boreas, and Pip watched with great curiosity as the bees grouped into a V-formation. As soon as they'd assembled, they flew off with great speed … in the direction of the Tower.

Mike's heartbeat increased with anticipation, as he suspected something unexpected was about to happen.

The bees - a squadron of the kingdom's elite Royal Air Force fighter pilots - came prepared for combat in flight jacket, helmet, and goggles. As they approached the Tower, Mike called out in amazement, "they're heading straight for the window." Boreas drifted to one side to allow them to pass, as Mike let go of his skateboard and ducked.

The bees flew through the open window and circled the cell before converging on the floor, where they regrouped in front of the skateboard.

"Wing Commander Hari Ha-ha here, sir," announced the squadron leader, saluting Mike. "Time is of the essence ... we have none to lose. Do you have any twine?"

Mike wondered for a moment. "In my backpack."

"Good," acknowledged the Wing Commander. "Mr Stitch mentioned you might have some. Cut four lengths and tie one to each wheel of the skateboard, then leave the rest to us," he instructed. "We're taking you for a flight."

The Wing Commander flew onto the nose of the skateboard to oversee the procedure.

Mike removed the string, bit off four lengths, then began attaching them to the wheels. Meanwhile, the bees formed into parallel lines on either side of the board.

Pip watched, fascinated, from the rafter.

"Welcome aboard Skate Air, flight 2106, non-stop service to Pembridge Town," announced the Wing Commander.

Mike scrambled onboard and promptly sat down on the deck.

"Why not join us?" Mike called up to Pip.

The bat was longing for something exciting to

happen in her life. The prospect of a little 'spirit of adventure' sounded too good an opportunity for her to pass up.

"Don't mind if I do," answered Pip as she opened her wings. "It sure beats hanging upside down all day."

Pip glided down from the rafter and landed onboard directly behind Mike.

Boreas watched in awe.

"All pilots take their positions," instructed the Wing Commander as he faced forward.

Each pilot lifted a section of string and gripped it tightly.

"Engines on ... prepare for lift-off," signalled Hari Ha-ha.

The pilots revved their engines in preparation for ascent.

"Lift after three," ordered the Wing Commander. "Three ... two ... one."

The skateboard slowly rose and hovered in the air.

"We have lift-off," announced the Wing Commander.

The look of dread on Wriggler's face was impossible to disguise.

At that precise moment, the sound of a key unlocking the cell door broke everyone's concentration.

Dawlok charged into the room. Raged by what he saw, he lashed out at the skateboard floating above his head, but it was too high for his reach.

"Antenna in the upright position," instructed the Wing Commander. "Engines full-on ... take flight."

Before Mike had time to button up his jacket, flight 2106 winged horizontally through the open window, out into the expansive blue sky.

"If we run into any difficulties with wind currents, you may have to blow us back on course," the Wing Commander called out to Boreas as they flew past.

Boreas winked and blew a gentle breath of air to help them on their way.

Flight 2106 swerved off into the open sky, looking unlike any other flying machine in the history of aviation. Dawlok, unable to pursue, leaned halfway out of the open window clenching his fists in a rage.

"Good afternoon, this is your Captain speaking," announced the Wing Commander. "On behalf of the crew, let me welcome you aboard Skate Air, flight 2106, non-stop service to Pembridge Town. The expected flight time is a little over two minutes. We should touchdown in Pembridge at 16:55 local time, depending on the headwind, assuming I can guide this contraption in the right direction. We've just hit our cruising altitude of 30 feet, and our speed is approximately 15 miles per hour. You'll notice I've turned off the 'Fasten Seatbelt' sign, which means you can now move freely about the cabin. However, please refasten them when you are seated for your own safety should we encounter any unexpected turbulence. Meanwhile, on behalf of your Captain and crew, please, relax and have a pleasant journey."

Down on the Avenue of Pembridge, animals, insects, and birds began to lift their heads aloft as they caught sight of the flying skateboard.

"Oh, what fun," remarked the Queen, excitedly, as she saw what she thought was the Royal Air Force performing an aerobatic display. Onlookers drew gasps of excitement as they too followed the Queen's gaze upwards and spotted the oddest-looking aircraft they had ever seen.

Flight 2106 gently tilted from side to side as it flew high above Pembridge Square and then turned in an arc to commence its gradual descent towards earth.

"This is your Captain speaking. We've begun our descent and will shortly be arriving at Pembridge International Airport. We trust you have enjoyed your flight and look forward to welcoming you again in the future. Please fasten your seatbelts," announced the Wing Commander "and prepare for landing."

"But I don't have one," yelped Wriggler as he

writhed inside Mike's pocket.

"Crew prepare for landing," ordered the Wing Commander.

"Ye Ha, Hari Ha-ha!" yelled Mike as he gripped both edges of the deck. "Hold on, Pip."

Pip was having such a great time, she had no intention of letting go and clung tightly to Mike's backpack.

Before anyone knew what was happening, flight 2106 was plummeting to earth with alarming speed.

The Wing Commander had lost control of the craft.

Luckily, Boreas was on hand. A gentle gust of wind helped break the board's descent and steered it safely to earth. The board landed with an abrupt thud on all four wheels on the Avenue of Pembridge, sending pedestrians running for their lives, before it taxied to a halt in a puddle of thick mud.

The forced landing threw everyone aboard onto the ground, slap-bang in front of Her Majesty the Queen. Mud splashed in every direction, including a large blob that smacked Lady Muck on her face.

The fighter pilots immediately regrouped into formation and then flew off back home to base, leaving Wing Commander Hari Ha-ha, Mike, Wriggler, and Pip behind in the square.

"Mud, glorious mud!" exclaimed Wriggler, from inside Mike's jacket pocket, as he peered out at the puddle of squishy mud spread out before him. "What I wouldn't do to bathe in that beauty at this very moment."

"Not you again," frowned the Queen, from behind her veil, gazing directly at Mike on the ground before her. "I thought you were locked away in the Tower!" She held her head aloft in disbelief. "I do so hate muck…"

"I presume YOU," interrupted Lady Muck, pointing at Mike, "are on your way to the courtroom, which is where we're all heading."

"Am I?" queried Mike as he decided it might be wiser to make a run for it.

"You can't park that, there," shouted a miserable jobsworth traffic warden, as she wriggled out from beneath the rear end of the skateboard and slapped a parking ticket on it. "It's on double-yellow lines … No parking at any time!" The bee then proceeded to point to two distinct yellow lines running across her jacket.

"Arrest that shrew at once," Lord Muck bellowed angrily.

"We've arrested him once already today," replied a member of the Royal Guard.

"Oh! Fiddlehead … just take him to court … and that's an order," fired Lord Muck. "And bring that aircraft, thingamabob with you ... and, his band of flying pirates."

"Really," grunted Lady Muck, as she removed a lace handkerchief from her sleeve and wiped the thick dollop of mud from her cheek. "You just couldn't make this up."

Before Mike had time to consider his options, members of the Royal Guard had surrounded him and his flying buddies.

"To the Court of Salazar, forthwith!" called out Lord Muck, waving his walking cane in the air.

"Welcome to Pembridge Town," announced the Wing Commander, as they were all led away, "and thank you for flying Skate Air."

CHAPTER 10

The Court of Salazar

"As odd as a bod can be,
he's odder than you or me.
As odd as a bod
that ever there was.
As odd as a bod can be."

So sang the court jester, an overly theatrical toad that was larger than a mouse, yet no bigger than a small grouse and whose job was to liven up the proceedings before the sombre business of the court commenced.

The jester of tricks, poetry, song, and little wisdom, wore a floppy three-cornered hat with an odd configuration of bells around it, matched with further bells upon his garish argyle-patterned tunic. The outfit clashed with his black and yellow hose and pointed black boots. He danced a silly jig waving ribbons in the air with bells attached to the ends as if to suggest the opening of a pageant or fair, not the start of a serious court case.

Many attendees in the public gallery dissolved into hysterics. Mike and Wriggler were sitting in the dock below next to Mike's barrister Mr Talkalot and glum-faced Wing Commander Hari Ha-ha and Pip. As Lord Chief Justice and judge, his eminence Lord Muck promptly banged his gavel down hard on the sounding block.

"Order! Order! You buffoon," he shouted sharply at the jester. "Order!"

Apart from the hiccupping duck sitting at the front of the spectators' gallery knitting a duck-egg blue slipper sock, the room fell quiet. The court was playing to a full house, for the gallery was packed to the rafters with every conceivable animal, insect, and bird that could fit into it.

"All rise," instructed the court tipstaff.

Everyone in the courtroom rose to their feet and bowed their head respectfully as Queen Beetrice entered, with Lady Muck in tow. The Queen took her place on a wooden throne positioned beneath the gallery, shielded from the gaze of the public. As soon as she was seated comfortably upon the thickly plumped, purple, velvet cushion, she rang a handbell to signify the trial could commence.

"We'll dispense with the formalities and push

forward with the business in hand," stated the judge, in haste, as if he was in a great hurry to get the case over and done with.

The Court of Salazar stood opposite the Tower on the eastern side of the square. It was named after a Portuguese dictator whose policies Queen Beetrice greatly admired. Salazar's state was established on the rigid principles of order, discipline, and authority. Opposition and criticism of the law were forbidden, and those who stepped out of line were swiftly imprisoned.

Wearing a short white wig, court coat, and long black silk gown, Lord Muck looked decidedly official sitting on his raised chair presiding over the courtroom. His eyes dropped as he consulted, casually at first, then with some interest, the greatly worded first page of the typed brief that rested on the bench in front of him. The words lay heavy upon the page. The courtroom remained silent during this procedure. After referring to it for several minutes, he put the document aside. Peering up from his half-rimmed spectacles, the Lord Chief Justice lifted his head and held his coat collar with two claws to address the jury and court.

It must be pointed out here and now before we continue that Pembridge's judicial system was unlike any other. It was devised so that the jury consisted of one member only, Her Majesty the Queen. As an absolute monarch, she determined all her subjects' fate, whether they were good or down the plughole bad. The reasoning behind this uncommon practice was simple; very little crime was committed in the kingdom. The tradition had worked effectively for centuries. There seemed no cause or reason for altering it.

The Queen's views and opinions were exact, as in the old-fashioned cast. She found modernism a hindrance to be avoided at all cost. To be fair, even though she was stuck in her ways, there was an element of truth in her beliefs. If it had worked well for thousands of years, why change merely for change's sake? As the Queen would often quote, "'tis better to leave things just as they are."

The court also had no registrar. The accused and witnesses were sworn in and out by separate oaths administered by the judge; the first oath was sworn on the bible before testimony was given. The second was declared under the QBO - the Queen's Beauty Oath - after giving evidence.

"Today's case is the Crown versus 'Too Bad' Mike," affirmed the judge sternly.

Handsome Cad was summoned to the witness box to be sworn in under oath. He promptly placed his left forepaw on the bible.

"Do you swear to tell the truth, the whole truth, and nothing but the truth?"

"I do," confirmed Cad with gritted teeth.

"With that determined, we can now move forward with the serious matter in hand." Lord Muck waved a foreclaw towards Mike's esteemed and veteran barrister, the talkative Mr Talkalot, a water vole.

"Would the counsel for the defence like to cross-examine the witness?"

"Yes, Your Honour."

Mr Talkalot stood and took his position in front of the court.

"Please inform the court of your name and occupation," requested Mr Talkalot.

"My name's Cad. I'm a footballer with Pembridge United Reserves."

"Mr Cad, we are here today to ascertain the ownership of a tail. Is the court right to assume you bought your second tail, the tail in question, from a tailor's shop, or were you born with two tails?"

The courtroom remained silent, apart from the hiccupping duck, as everyone awaited Cad's reply.

"I bought my second tail from a market stall in Pembridge Square that sells the latest designer wear at knock-down prices," Cad spoke confidently.

All the crow reporters in the press enclosure scribbled down his reply on their notepads.

"And who owns the said stall in Pembridge Square?" asked the barrister, inquisitively.

"Spiv, the water shrew," responded Cad, without delay.

"That will be all, My Lord," Mr Talkalot informed the judge. The barrister returned to his seat.

"Would the counsel for the prosecution care to question his client, Mr Cad," the judge asked the barrister Mr Littletalk, who was also a water vole.

Unluckily for Cad, he had drawn the short straw and been assigned the junior and most inexperienced barrister on the counsel, who until now had never represented anyone in court.

"No, Your Honour, that won't be necessary," replied Mr Littletalk, while referring to his thick brief on the table in front of him.

"In that case, Mr Cad…"

"Yes, Your Honour?" interrupted Cad.

"It falls upon me to swear you out by asking you the QBO."

This he did.

"In your humble opinion, is Her Majesty Queen Beetrice, ruler of the kingdom of Pembridge, the most beautiful female in the land?"

The judge asked the question with a seriousness that befitted his role as Lord Chief Justice.

The room froze with anticipation as everyone

awaited Cad's response.

"Yes, Your Honour. The Queen is more beautiful than a thousand sweet-smelling roses rich in summer pollen."

Queen Beetrice was somewhat taken aback by his poetic reply. From behind her veil, she curiously curled her tiny lips before raising an arched eyebrow in wonderment. She then gave a serene wave of gratitude that lasted all of two seconds. Of course, no one in the courtroom saw this gesture because everyone was forbidden to look at her. However, there was one animal who noticed. That animal was Wriggler, who was sneakily watching everything from Mike's denim jacket top pocket.

Several female spectators in the gallery swooned and fluttered their eyelashes in Cad's direction.

"That, Her Majesty is beauty personified," barked the judge, addressing the room as though he were an authority on the attributes and subtleties of beauteous matters, "is a fact not to be contested."

Supporters of the monarchy applauded and cheered in wild agreement waving perfumed handkerchiefs and stiff brimmed hats in the air. Conversely, upon hearing Cad's declaration, the hiccupping duck remained emotionless while continuing to knit her sock.

"Order! Order!" The judge hit his wooden gavel

with authority on the sounding block. The room returned to a resemblance of respectability.

"Mr Cad, you may leave the witness box," instructed the judge.

Cad left the stand with a stride in his step and returned to his seat beside his barrister.

"Bring forth exhibit A," requested the judge.

Without delay, the court jester crossed the floor and stood in front of the house. He held up a short black tail so the whole courtroom could see it.

"Yes … a tail," the judge confirmed to the bemused members of the spectators' gallery.

The barrister Mr Talkalot rose from his seat with poise and addressed the judge.

"May I call a witness for the prosecution to the stand, Your Honour?"

"Proceed," directed the judge.

An East End water shrew - Cad's sidekick - rigged-out in the latest fashionable sportswear entered the courtroom and was escorted to the witness box. He removed his baseball cap, placed his left forepaw on the bible, and was duly sworn in under oath.

"Please inform the court of your name and occupation," requested Mr Talkalot.

"The name's Spiv … I own a market stall in Pembridge Square."

"And am I correct in saying you know Mr Cad, and

if so, how?"

"Sure do," he shook his head rather smugly. "He's one of my regular customers."

"And am I also correct in saying the latest fashion on the street is for males to wear TWO tails?"

Several male spectators in the public gallery cheered approvingly.

"The word on the page says two tails are all the rage," rapped Spiv. He played to the spectators' gallery like a seasoned performer.

"And would I also be correct in stating you stock such tails on your stall and that you sold one to Mr Cad?"

"The word in the 'hood is
I stock the best designer goods,
Fermés, B&E, and Jeantier,
and lots more fashionable branded wear.
By the looks of that tail on display,
I reckon it's seen better days.
There's no label attached to its girth.
In my opinion, for what it's worth,
I'd say it was a cheap imitation,
'cause I know how to dress the nation."

So rapped Spiv in his broad East End accent.

Gasps of surprise and disbelief spread across the

public gallery. Spiv's testimony struck a discordant note with Cad's harmonious turn of events.

A worried-looking Cad quickly conferred with his barrister. His lead witness was not playing according to their plan.

"A cheap imitation,
well, listen to that.
If I didn't know better
I'd eat my hat."

And so the silly court jester ad-libbed amid all the incredulity while still holding the tail in question up in the air.

Mike leaped up from his seat to protest. "I'll have you know, Your Honour, my tail is not a cheap imitation. It's the finest shrew's tail in the kingdom."

"Objection!" called out the judge angrily. "Speak only when you are spoken to."

"The finest of tails
you ever did see.
If I sat an exam,
I'd have a degree."

And so the daft court jester continued to improvise, impervious to official court etiquette.

"Order! Order! You witless clown, Order!" demanded the judge. As he pounded his gavel hard on the sounding block, it woke up Miss Chief - the moth, stenographer, and wiz shorthand typist - from snatching a late afternoon nap. Unbeknown to her, upon waking, she accidentally knocked the transcript she'd been typing off her desk into the wastepaper basket.

A resemblance of normality was quickly restored, and the questioning resumed.

"Am I to understand that you categorically did not sell the tail in question to Mr Cad?" maintained Mr Talkalot, bluntly.

"Coooooorrect," upheld Spiv as he clicked two fingers with precision.

Cad turned his gaze towards the floor. His defence was descending into disarray.

"Allow me to rephrase the last question I put to you, Mr Cad," asked the barrister, as he held his forefeet behind his back. "Am I, therefore, to assume such a tail could not be bought on your market stall?"

"I only sell the best counterfeit merchandise. I never touch the rest," Spiv freely confessed.

Laughter splattered across the spectators' gallery.

"Quiet please," ordered the judge as he brought down his gavel on top of his thick paged brief by mistake.

"May I remind you, Mr Spiv, you are in a court of law, and this is a grave matter," the judge issued his warning sternly.

"I apologize, My Lord, I got a bit carried away," Spiv grinned to himself. "It won't happen again, I assure you."

"Good … Make sure it doesn't," sighed the judge.

The Queen shuffled her numerous feet restlessly to show her growing boredom with the tedious toing and froing of the questioning. To occupy her mind, she delved into her chocolate box, which she'd conveniently concealed beneath her long gold and black embroidered cloak.

"That will be all, Your Honour," Mr Talkalot affirmed to the judge. The barrister returned to his seat.

"Would the counsel for the prosecution care to cross-examine the witness, Mr Spiv?" enquired the judge.

"Err, no, no, that won't be necessary, Your Honour," replied Mr Littletalk. He was frantically referring to his thick brief on the table in front of him, trying to comprehend what line of questioning he should take up.

Spiv was sworn out under the QBO and escorted from the courtroom looking rather smug.

At this point, a boisterous interruption occurred in

the spectators' gallery at the rear. A group of latecomers had arrived. Everyone in the courtroom, except the Queen, whose view was restricted, turned to see who was causing the disturbance.

Amid the commotion, pushing his way to the front of the balcony was Grandfather Gus. Mike's spirit immediately lifted. He leaned over and informed his barrister that his lead witness had just turned up. Mr Talkalot scribbled the information upon his brief and circled an inscription beside it that read, 'character witness.'

"Order! Quiet in the gallery," the judge called, as a sprightly, young hedgehog relinquished his front-row seat for Grandfather Gus to occupy.

The next witness, a water rat, was called to the stand and sworn in under oath.

"Would the counsel for the defence like to question the witness?" enquired the judge.

"Yes, Your Honour," confirmed Mr Talkalot. He crossed over to the stand clutching his brief.

"Please confirm your name and occupation," requested Mr Talkalot.

"I'm Dodger ... a self-employed wheeler-dealer."

"Ah! Mr Dodger," said the barrister, with ripened glee in his voice, while flicking to the appropriate page in his brief. "Am I correct in believing you are here today as a character witness for Mr Cad?" The barrister placed great emphasis upon the word 'character' as he asked the question.

"Correct," announced Dodger, proudly.

"And am I also right in saying that you, Mr Dodger, were taking bets today at the summer fête on whether the tail in question was genuine or not?" The barrister pelted the words out with incredulity.

"Still am, sir ... Ten to one, it's a fake," replied Dodger, keenly.

"Really!" remarked the judge, with great interest. "That's excellent odds. I'll put a tenner on." He suddenly realized what he'd said and corrected himself immediately.

"Objection!" cautioned the judge. "Really, whatever next? Gambling of any description is strictly forbidden in this courtroom."

"Sorry, My Lord," apologised Dodger. "It won't happen again."

"Yes, well, where were we?" enquired the judge, as he straightened the collar on his coat.

The Queen's interest in the trial was noticeably sagging. In her mind, this was nutritious snacking time she'd had to renounce. She leaned sideward and requested a tumbler of water from Lady Muck to wash down a particularly gooey caramel filling she was having difficulty swallowing.

Dodger had played straight into the paws of Mr

Talkalot and openly humiliated himself. The judge, counsel, public, and, most importantly, the jury would never now take him seriously as a witness.

Mr Talkalot closed his brief and turned to face the judge. "I have no further questions to ask Mr Dodger."

"In that case," replied the judge, "would the counsel for the defence care to cross-examine the witness?"

"Err, no, no, that won't be necessary," replied Mr Littletalk. The barrister was anxiously searching the index of his leather-bound copy of *The Common Laws of Pembridge* for guidance.

Dodger was sworn out under the QBO and escorted, with his tail firmly between his legs, back to his seat.

Cad's frustration increased with each witness that appeared. His best and last line of defence had now been ridiculed. If he was to clear his name, a significant turn of evidence in his favour had to materialise from somewhere.

The judge referred to the lengthy worded brief on his bench before speaking next.

"Will Mr … 'Too Bad' Mike, please take the stand."

"My name is Mike, not 'Too Bad,'" protested Mike loudly as he was escorted to the box.

"Objection!" insisted the judge, who looked quite put out by Mike's persistence. "Speak only when you are spoken to."

"Whatever," shrieked Wriggler as he snuck out of view inside Mike's top pocket.

Mike peered up at his grandfather in the spectators' gallery as if to garner support. He then placed his paw on the bible and was sworn in under oath.

The judge called out to Mr Littletalk, "Would the counsel for the defense care to question 'Too Bad' Mike?"

Mr Littletalk lifted his head from the leather-bound copy of *The Common Laws of Pembridge* and, to everyone's surprise, responded, "Yes, Your Honour." He shut the manual, stood up, and crossed over to the stand.

Mr Littletalk's line of questioning would take on a new, fresh approach, namely, to trick the accused into admitting his guilt. For a moment, he fumbled for words, then showered them out in a spray.

"How much did you pay for the tail in question," he asked, bluntly, to try and trip Mike up.

Mike kept his cool and remained calm.

"I was born without a tail, so my grandmother made me one, which happens to be the finest tail in the land." Mike paused momentarily for effect and then continued, "the tail was a gift and is priceless."

When the Queen heard the word 'priceless,' she glanced at the lavender chocolate she was nibbling with sudden distaste and dropped it half-eaten. She had suddenly lost interest in snacking. Her interest in the trial, however, had sharpened as it took on a curious twist. She leaned forward in her throne to get a clearer look at Mike. For some reason, she felt sure she'd seen the shrew somewhere else that same day before the unpleasant incident occurred at that afternoon's summer fête. For the life of her, though, she could not remember where.

When the hiccupping duck in the spectators' gallery heard Mike's declaration, she also did something unheard of and dropped a stitch. If her memory served her well, she'd taught Mike's grandmother to sew and knew all about the tail she'd made for her grandson.

The barrister continued his line of interrogation.

"And what, in your opinion, constitutes a good tail?" Mr Littletalk's grilling was becoming more thrilling by the second.

A fair and interesting point decided the judge as he slowly nodded his head in accord.

Mike thought long and hard before answering the question.

"A middle, an end, and a beginning," he confidently informed the court.

"*The tail is a fake,*

for heaven's sake.
The accused got a grilling.
Isn't this thrilling,
a middle, an end, and a beginning."

So sang the camp jester while thrusting the tail in question with both forefeet higher into the air.

"Order! Order! You ridiculously incompetent toad," shouted the judge, harshly. "Right, where were we?" he flapped.

"An end ... a beginning ... and a middle, Your Honour," replied Mr Littletalk, in a muddle.

"Yes, yes, we've been through all that. Let's just proceed with the case, shall we!" The judge waved his gavel in exasperation.

Dodger, the wheeler-dealer, was always looking for new angles to attract more business. He promptly stood up and yelled across to Mike. "I could have got you a tail much cheaper than that and thrown in a pair of trainers and a baseball hat at no extra cost," he bragged, deviously.

Mike could smell a rat. This long-tailed rodent wasn't known for his generosity.

"Objection!" called out the judge with irritation.

"I'm happy with the tail I had; it fits the bum I've got," exclaimed Mike, in retaliation. "It's bespoke, and I can guarantee, as twelve is a shilling, the tail in question belongs to me." That bit of testimony hit Dodger way below the belt.

"The tail is for real,
it has such appeal.
If twelve is a shilling,
I'm counting my winnings.
A middle, an end, and a beginning ... I'm sending my bill in."

So sang the overly theatrical jester who, in his excitement, began ringing his bells.

"Order! Order! You blockhead," shouted the judge angrily as his cheeks began to redden. The jester quietened down.

Mr Littletalk resumed his questioning a little more cautiously, well, so he thought!

"Exactly what evidence do you have to suggest Mr Cad acquired the tail in question, dishonestly?"

This was a leading question if ever there was one, and one that should have by rights been objected to by the judge. Surprisingly it wasn't.

Mike answered the question precisely and descriptively with clarity in his voice.

"After I awoke this morning and discovered my tail was missing, I found a distinctive set of footprints at my lair in Colville Hollow that led all the way to

Pembridge Creek. From there, the trail crossed to Hollow Twine and beyond to Pembridge Town." He spoke slowly to emphasize the relevant points. Everyone in the courtroom listened intently. "The footprints were quite unique. The right forefoot had four clawed toes, while the other three feet had five. As everybody knows, unlike a mouse that has four toes on its front feet and five on its hind, shrews have five clawed toes on all four feet."

Mike drew in a deep breath and fell quiet for a few moments to allow everyone in the courtroom time to digest this intriguing piece of testimony.

Smoke rose from the crow reporter's pencils as they frantically scribbled down his statement like crazed gerbils on a Ferris wheel.

At this point, Commander Hari Ha-ha stood up requesting to speak, but Mr Talkalot, knowing full well he'd have been in contempt of court, motioned him back down into his seat.

Grandfather Gus peered from the gallery at Mike and nodded approvingly to encourage him to continue.

Mike did, but this time he addressed the judge directly.

"I should like to request, Your Honour, that Mr Cad be given a paw inspection to determine how many toes he has on his right forepaw."

"Objection!" Mr Littletalk called out, furiously.

A look of surprise flashed across the judge's face as he wondered why the barrister should feel the need to object.

In the gallery, spectators began to shuffle uneasily in their seats, indicating their disapproval at the barrister's intervention.

The judge observed their unrest, and purposely took his time responding, enjoying the spotlight. After several moments of deliberation, he spoke.

"Objection … overruled," the judge conceded, in an attempt to appease the growing discontent in the air.

By rights, a judge should remain impartial during a case, but Lord Muck had clearly sided with Cad. Everyone attending knew if Cad's front paw had only four toes, this fact alone would add considerable weight to Mike's evidence. To counteract this eventuality, the judge devised a little scheme to aid Cad should the need arise. The judge put forward a suggestion to the court.

"This is a most unusual request from 'Too Bad' Mike," he spoke with caution in his voice. "However, in light of the circumstances, I will grant such an inspection, to be carried out forthwith, by myself."

The judge rose from his chair, left the bench, and crossed the floor. Everyone in the courtroom watched his every step.

On the face of it, Cad was seemingly cornered.

The Queen lifted her left eyebrow as an inkling of mistrust entered her mind in surprise at this sudden deviation from court procedure.

"Surely, Your Honour," she swiftly intervened to correct him, "as I am the jury, such evidence should also be made available for me to inspect?"

Her words halted the judge in his tracks, for when the Queen spoke, he had, by law, to comply. His little scheme to tamper with the evidence had backfired.

"Why, of course, Your Majesty," the judge replied somewhat reluctantly, as he bowed his head.

Cad was duly instructed to hold out his right forepaw and turn his head away from view so the judge and jury could observe the evidence.

After the inspection, Queen Beetrice and the judge returned to their respective seats without uttering a word or making any indication of what they had just observed.

The questioning resumed.

"'Too Bad' Mike … do you really expect the court to believe you've spent the whole day chasing your own tail?" Mr Littletalk's quizzing hit Mike straight between the eyes. "I find the notion utterly absurd."

"Well," said Mike, hesitantly, "if you put it like that … yes!"

The court fell about laughing.

"Why, if we all spent the day chasing our own tail, we'd never get anything done," mocked the barrister. "I rest my case, Your Honour; the accused is obviously a thief and wasting valuable court time."

The judge took note of this interesting fact. "Will that be all," he asked Mr Littletalk civilly.

The barrister looked wholly relieved at having conducted his first cross-examination. "I have no further questions, Your Honour." He shuffled back to his seat, pleased the ordeal was over.

"Would the counsel for the defence like to question his client, 'Too Bad' Mike?"

"I would, Your Honour," answered Mr Talkalot. The barrister crossed over to the stand.

"Mike ... am I correct in believing you would be able to recognize your missing tail in an instance?"

"Yes."

"And is the tail, known as exhibit A, that tail?"

"It is," answered Mike positively.

Mr Talkalot turned to face the judge. "That will be all, Your Honour. I have no further questions to ask."

Mike remained in the witness box as his barrister returned to his seat.

The Queen, counsel, public, and most markedly, the judge sank into their seats with relief in the fulfilling knowledge the trial was nearing its completion. Although, to be exact, everyone was still unsure which way the case would go.

CHAPTER 11

The Verdict

The judge closed the thickly paged memorandum on the bench in front of him and cleared his throat to address the court.

"We've heard compelling evidence today from the accused and various witnesses with regards to the tail in question. It now leaves me with one final duty to perform, to swear 'Too Bad' Mike out under the QBO." He cleared his throat once more. "'Too Bad' Mike, in your humble opinion, is Her Majesty Queen Beetrice, ruler of the kingdom of Pembridge, the most beautiful female in the land?" The judge crossed his forelegs to await Mike's reply.

For the first time during the case, Mike felt unsure how he should respond. At the back of his mind, he recalled what his grandad had told him when he was knee-high to a grasshopper, "Whatever you do in life, do it with honesty in your heart."

With that thought in mind and with all the courage

he could muster inside his heart, Mike answered the question truthfully.

"My grandad brought me up never to lie," he informed the judge. "Endeavour to be the best you can be; that's what my grandad taught me."

Apart from the hiccupping duck, everyone in the room fell as silent as a broken grandfather clock.

Mike continued.

"Her Majesty clearly was once the most beautiful female in the land, but time has taken its course, and now her beauty is but a memory, reminiscent of a long distant friend."

No one in the courtroom could believe what their ears had just heard. How could this lowly shrew, whom hardly anyone knew before being brought in front of the court, have so blatantly and indignantly insulted Her Majesty ... and so publicly!

Unaware, Mike had opened a hornet's nest.

"Off with his head," came a clamorous yell from the back of the public gallery. The courtroom exploded into a babel of catcalls and chants as almost everyone rose to their feet and called out unanimously, "Off with his head, off with his head, off with his head."

That was, apart from the hiccupping duck who carried on regardless, knitting her sock, and Grandfather Gus and his associates who lowered their heads in shame. How could Mike have spoken so disrespectfully about the Queen? Grandfather Gus was at an utter loss to comprehend.

"The court is a mess.
Whoever would guess?
There's little decorum.
It's madness. Ignore them.
The court is a mess.
Whoever would guess?
Just look at the judge,
a finger of fudge.
The court is a mess.
Off with his head.
Whoever would ever have guessed?"

So sang the nutty court jester amid all the madness.

"Order! Order! You idiotic toad," yelled the judge in a futile attempt to regain control.

"Treason … The shrew is in contempt of court. He's clearly a fool!" claimed Mr Littletalk.

Mike listened in disbelief as onlookers threw words of scorn at him.

Amid the brouhaha, the Queen did not stir a single hair or muscle upon her body. Her appearance would have been recorded in the reporter's notebooks, were they allowed to observe her, as being one of genteel and dignified repose.

"Order! Order!" yelled the judge, once more, as he repeatedly banged his gavel hard upon the sounding block. "Order!"

The courtroom slowly regained a sense of authority as silence returned.

The judge lifted his head heavenward as if he was summoning guidance from his maker. Just as he was about to make a statement, Queen Beetrice unexpectedly interrupted the proceedings.

"Pass me a mirror, forthwith," she beckoned to her Lady of the Bedchamber.

Lady Muck opened her leather court bag and rummaged through it before plucking out a small circular mirror, which she duly passed to Her Majesty.

The Queen lifted the veil from her face and studied her image momentarily in the mirror. Several uneasy seconds passed before she spoke.

"Why ... 'Too Bad' Mike is correct." She placed the mirror down and rose from her throne to speak directly to the judge.

"It is true ... like the evening sunlight, my looks have faded. In my opinion, I believe Mike is not bad at all. He does not lie, unlike some, I could mention in this courtroom."

Queen Beetrice turned to face the gallery. She then did the one thing she had never been permitted to do during her entire reign as a monarch, to face her public and address them.

A hush of disbelief enveloped the spectator's gallery as all eyes focused on the Queen.

"From this moment onward, I will no longer hide behind a mask. I may be weathered and curvaceous, but I am your Queen, and I am proud to be so."

Muffled rumblings of shock and amazement rippled throughout the gallery as everyone jostled for a closer view of Her Majesty.

"The Queen is weathered.
Who would have thought it!
A face like a ball,
a ball you can bat.
The Queen is curvaceous.
Who would have imagined!
A body like cake,
the chocolate she ate.
The Queen is voracious.
Whoever would ever have guessed?"

So sang the delirious court jester who could barely contain his glee at the confusion that surrounded him.

"Order! Order! You scuttlebutt," screamed the judge, as he frantically tried to summon a semblance of protocol back into the courtroom.

> *"The judge is a fool.*
> *a one-legged stool.*
> *In my opinion,*
> *I think we should bin him.*
> *The trial is a sham.*
> *All pickle and ham.*
> *The law is an ass,*
> *and nobody knows who I am."*

"Order! Order! You dunderhead," yelled the judge, while repeatedly banging his gavel with such force it broke the sounding block in half. "Members of the public, please … ORDER!"

All the spectator's, apart from the hiccupping duck, finally fell silent.

The Queen regained her regal stance and repositioned herself back on her throne. The judge quietly placed the gavel down on the bench as if it was more fragile than a precious piece of crystal. He then wiped his sweated brow with a white handkerchief and addressed the Queen.

"Has the jury reached a unanimous verdict, Your Majesty?" he asked slowly and precisely.

"The jury has, Your Honour," proclaimed the Queen, as she gracefully gathered her frock and stood back up to address the court.

This she did with great dignity.

"After much deliberation, the jury has reached a unanimous decision. But before I announce the verdict, I should like to say a few words to all those assembled here today."

The Queen crossed to the centre of the floor so everyone could see her.

"A shrew without a tail … is like a bride without a veil. The two go together like honey and bees."

She gazed up towards the many heads in the gallery.

"It's impossible to put a value on intangible things, such as clouds or thin air. The same can be said for trust, truth, and integrity; they're priceless qualities. All the tangible things in life become worthless when compared to these values. Using this principle, the jury's verdict is as such."

There followed a short, determined pause before she continued.

"It is factually true that Mr Cad has four toes on his right forepaw, but that evidence in itself does not necessarily point the claw of blame at him. How he came by the said tail, we will probably never know. If he did steal it, then hopefully, this court case will have taught him a lesson. That said, it is the jury's belief the said tail rightfully belongs to 'Too Bad'

Mike, for he is the only honest person in this courtroom."

Uneasy gasps from those with a guilty conscience echoed about the room.

The judge intervened to ascertain the jury's ruling of the official charge, "Does the jury find the accused, 'Too Bad' Mike, guilty of theft ma'am?"

She turned to face him. "NOT GUILTY! Your Honour."

Almost everyone in the courtroom, including Handsome Cad and the malignant Lady Muck, rose from their seats in dissent, fiercely protesting their honesty and integrity.

"Order! Order!" called out the Queen at the top of her voice to calm the unruliness. "This is not a circus! … Bring me the tail this instance," she instructed the judge.

"Of course, ma'am," replied the grovelling judge, as he motioned to the jester. "The accused is acquitted. The tail must be reunited with its rightful owner at once."

All eyes fell on the court jester as he held the tail up into the air for all to see.

"Cad is a liar,
he has four toes.
The tail in question,

he must forgo.
The accused is acquitted.
The jury's united.
Let justice be done.
The wrong has been righted."

So sang the court jester with a spring in his step as he crossed the courtroom to lay the tail upon the soft, plump velvet cushion in front of the Queen's throne.

"Would Mike, please step forward," requested the Queen.

Mike left the witness box and stood before Her Majesty.

"Please accept the Court of Salazar's sincere apology for the inconvenience and dismay you have endured, and may I offer you and your friends as recompense an invitation to attend tonight's banquet at Hive Castle ... as my guests of honour."

The Queen leaned forward and offered Mike the return of his tail. As she did, she whispered closely in his ear.

"Was it a fluke you answered the QBO so truthfully ... or did you perchance take a peep at me this morning during my constitutional?"

The Queen never forgot a face.

Before Mike had time to reply, the Queen leaned back and let out a raucous laugh, relieved finally to have met the first honest person in her kingdom.

In the turn of the moment, Mike grabbed a passing Samson snail, slapped a dollop of extra strong glue on his behind, and finally reunited the tail with his rear.

"Liberate all prisoners in the Tower, forthwith," ordered the Queen, "and invite them to the banquet."

A division of Royal Guards was dispatched directly to the Tower.

"All rise," instructed the court tipstaff.

The Queen gathered her long gold and black embroidered cloak about her, and just as she was about to depart, turned to Mike. "I'll see you later, at the banquet." She left the building in fits of laughter, followed closely by an austere looking Lady Muck.

"Case dismissed," acknowledged the judge, curtly, as he closed the trial with a final and swift bang of the gavel.

After the court had been cleared of all its spectators', a cleaner entered to tidy up. She emptied all the wastepaper baskets into a large rubbish bag and, in the process, unwittingly threw away the only copy of Miss Chief's case transcript.

The significance of the Queen's speech in court today would have far-reaching ramifications throughout the kingdom of Pembridge, none more so than for Lord and Lady Muck. Her faith in the judicial system had been significantly undermined. It was time for a major reform and shake-up of the legal constitution, which she would focus upon in the coming weeks. In the meantime, the Queen had more enjoyable things to attend, primarily this evening's summer banquet.

The Tail of 'Too Bad' Mike

CHAPTER 12

The Grand Banquet

Summer Fête Banquet
Menu

Sunflower honey soup with beebread

Honeyed stems with honeydew melon

Half-baked honey beechnut roast with
mustard and thyme honey marinade

Salad leaves, sliced runner beans
and beetroot with herb vinaigrette

Royal jelly and chocolate blancmange
with milk thistle-ice cream

Pembridge white nectar wine
or Pembridge red nectar wine

The banqueting hall glistened with warm shimmering light from the huge drop crystal chandeliers and table candelabras. Their reflection gleamed upon the highly waxed walls. The diligence and flair of Mrs Washalot and the hard graft she encouraged from her army of worker bees had paid off tenfold. Redolent with white and yellow honeysuckle, the room looked more splendid than she could ever have hoped for.

The castle interior was colossal and housed a small city. Visiting guests could easily get lost inside its complex and densely packed matrix of hexagonal rooms and winding passages. Those guests who flew in for the event landed on the roof helipad and were directed by a guard down twenty flights of stairs to the ground floor's banqueting hall. Invitations had been posted to two hundred guests and clearly stipulated 'evening dress.' In a bid to get noticed by the Queen, everyone attending came dressed to the nines wearing their finest garments.

A fanfare of trumpets greeted the Queen as she made her entrance, followed by spontaneous applause from her guests. She wore a simple, floor-length, gold-coloured gown with short diaphanous sleeves, embellished with a dazzling necklace and bejewelled crown. As she walked to the table, she briefly cast her eyes around the room in admiration at the elaborate decorations as if to give her royal nod of approval. Preceding her were her guests of honour, Mike (with Wriggler in his jacket pocket), Grandfather Gus, and Pip. To everyone's amusement and delight, Mike had also dressed specially for the occasion and was wearing two tails, his own and the fine red tail Mr Stitch had made for him.

In a break from protocol, Queen Beetrice requested to be seated in the centre of the table, beside Mike and his friends.

Surprisingly, in a further breach of procedure, Lord and Lady Muck were banished to the far, far end of the table, beneath the minstrel gallery, away from any high-ranking officials. Their influence was deemed redundant now that the Queen had turned over a new leaf.

Before the sumptuous feast commenced, as customary, the Queen delivered a speech.

"I am delighted to welcome my honoured guests Mike, Wriggler, Grandfather Gus, and Pip to Hive Castle. Since my accession to the throne, I have tried with utmost determination to be a just and fair monarch and to rule as my forbearers have done. However, that has not always been as straight forward as I would have hoped. I feel I have, at times, allowed my better judgement to be unwisely influenced. The time for a change now beckons.

Tonight I would like you to join me in celebrating this momentous occasion and this happy milestone in Pembridge's history. My Lords, Ladies, and Gentlefolk, may I ask you all to rise and drink a toast to Mike, Grandfather Gus, and their friends."

The guests rose from their seats, clutching a glass of nectar wine, and clinched the toast.

After the tribute, the toastmaster intervened and sounded two chinks with a spoon on his wine glass. The room fell silent as he also proposed a toast.

"Three cheers for Her Majesty … hip, hip."

"Hurrah," called out the guests.

"Hip, hip."

"Hurrah."

"Hip, hip."

"Hurrah."

"Long live the Queen," they cheered in unison before toasting her health.

At six-thirty sharp, a gong sounded, and the banquet commenced. Cuisine to gorge one's eyes on was laid upon the table. Mike, Grandfather Gus, Pip, and Wriggler, who had his own plate to eat from, scoffed everything put in front of them, as did the ravenous Queen.

The feast took all of half an hour to devour. To accompany the meal, the Pembridge Symphony Orchestra seated in the minstrel gallery played all

four movements of the specially commissioned
Symphony for Wind. The music harmonised perfectly
with the mood of the occasion and helped drown out
the cacophony of burps, belches, slurping, gulping,
and other such bodily noises that emanated from the
diners.

Seated below the minstrel gallery, in-between Lord
and Lady Muck at the far, far end of the banqueting
table, was the peg-nosed councillor, Mr Bytheway, a
stink bug. He smelt as if he'd never washed in his
entire life - in practice, he probably hadn't. His odour
was so pungent, one sniff could knock you out cold.
He worked for the Highways and Byways
Transportation Department at Pembridge town hall
and was a terrible bore.

As soon as the Mucks discovered they were sitting
beside him, they immediately requested pegs from a
foot servant and promptly clipped them tightly to
their nostrils.

"By the way, remind me to buy you a bar of soap
this Christmas," snarled Lady Muck to the councillor.

"I never eat the stuff," replied the smelly stink bug,
who seemed totally unconcerned by her rudeness. "It
lays heavy on the lips." He leaned over the table and
picked up a plate of beebread, and offered her a slice.

"No, thank you, I never eat the stuff," replied Lady

Muck. "It weighs heavy on the hips."

Lord and Lady Muck were adamant; they did not
intend to be ostracised from court duties. They did,
after all, hold titles bestowed upon them for life by
the Queen. Such titles came with all the privileges
and customs they'd grown accustomed to. Also, Lord
Muck knew full well no law ordained courtesy titles
could be revoked.

Their disdain for Mike grew the moment he won
favour with the Queen. They held him solely
responsible for their fall from grace. To regain the
Queen's trust, they would somehow have to
dishonour him. Quite how they were to do this, they
had yet to grasp. For the moment, they decided it
might be judicious to lie low until the dust from
today's events had settled. To their advantage, they
still operated a network of spies, the MIO - Muck
Intelligence Organisation. One of its principal
members was Dawlok, who was now theoretically
unemployed since all the Tower of the Wind's
internees had been released.

For the moment, the Queen had more enjoyable
things to occupy her mind. She would decide the
Mucks fate at a later date. For now, she was content
to have them grovel a little. After all, it is far wiser to
keep one's enemy within earshot lest they should

plan a revolt

The banquet was a great success and scoffed in record time. It was noted by several guests how well Queen Beetrice and Grandfather Gus were getting along.

"How did you arrive," she asked, "by the river?"

"Yes, by raft. I built it myself. It's called *Titanic.*"

"Rafting! ... how exciting. I have a Royal Barge I inherited from my mother, the old Queen. It chugs along slower than a stickleback," she laughed, "much like she used to. So I can call you, Captain Gus, can I?"

"By all means, ma'am... everyone else does when I'm sailing."

"Talking of the old Queen," she called to mind, "I'm having a memorial rockery built on the south-west corner of the square to commemorate her. I ordered a consignment of stones from the downs. They may as well be coming from Antarctica, the amount of time they're taking to get here."

"I've always had an eye for an attractive rockery," revealed Grandfather Gus.

The Queen looked quite taken aback by his comment and appeared to blush. "You really must visit Pembridge Town more often," she insisted.

"I would if I didn't suffer from such bad flatulence,"

explained Grandfather Gus, "and keep dozing off."

"Oh! That's nothing," pooh-hoed the Queen, as she broke wind. "I suffer from heavy legs, and I still manage to get around."

"Really! ... Now that's an ailment you don't hear of very often."

To round the evening off, a series of entertainments had been arranged in the adjoining open-air amphitheatre. The show's producer, Cebee Demille, an awkward, gangly crane fly, arrived on the stage to introduce the first performer.

"Your Majesty, my Lords, Ladies and Gentlefolk, tonight's show will commence with an excerpt from Prokofiev's *Romeo and Juliet*. Please welcome on stage, Miss Tatiana Delphinium, who will dance the balcony pas de deux, solo."

A warm round of applause filled the air as the orchestra played the opening bars of the score. However, after playing the introduction repeatedly, there was still no entrance by the dancer.

Mr Demille scoured backstage for the missing ballerina.

"You there!" he called out to a figure hovering by a wing. "You're late!" He then flew over and pushed the dancer out on to the stage.

Gasps of astonishment greeted her entrance.

Unfortunately, in his haste, Mr Demille had pushed the hiccupping duck on stage in error. Thinking her full-length woolly socks to be a leotard, he presumed she was the temperamental white dove ballerina Tatiana Delphinium, a Principal of the Royal Ballet. Mrs Quack had mistakenly strayed backstage after visiting the ladies room to powder her beak. Looking more flabbergasted than the audience, all she could do was stand and hiccup.

"I do so love Prokofiev. *Romeo and Juliet* is my favourite ballet," whispered the Queen into Grandfather Gus's ear. "Though I always thought the piece was composed for a pair of courting doves … not a single duck!"

Grandfather Gus had no idea of any of it. It was all news to him.

"Do something," the producer called out frantically to the duck. "Pirouette … or something … Do a jeté."

And how the audience roared, as the duck attempted a spin, and then another. Her whirls kept spinning off in the wrong direction, for her feet were far too large and flat for delicate ballet moves.

The producer flew on stage in a bid to dampen the audience's hilarity and stopped the show. "Just a hiccup," he addressed the guests, "merely a temporary setback, I assure you."

"How blooming annoying," interjected the Queen.

"Muffle the sound, dear duck," injected a high-ranking guest. "Don't you know it's socially unacceptable behaviour!"

Poor Mrs Quack didn't know which way to look.

"How do you cure hiccups?" asked a guest, inquisitively.

"Oh! What fun," interrupted the Queen. "A game … how to cure hiccups."

"A Boo! A surprise, a shock or a fright usually does the trick," called out a guest.

"Suck on a lemon," yelled another.

"Drink a glass of water upside down," insisted Pip, who was hanging upside down from a ledge.

"Drink from the wrong side of a glass," suggested a rather inebriated guest.

"Put your knees up to your chest and pull on your tongue," advised another.

"A spoonful of sugar soaked in malt vinegar," recommended Madame Petronella.

This was all getting too out of hand for the producer. He motioned the duck off stage and introduced the next entertainer.

"Flown in, especially for the occasion and at great expense, please give a huge Pembridge welcome for the international soprano, Miss Sarah B., singing her worldwide hit 'Deliver Me.'"

The warbling canary appeared like an apparition

through a cloud of dry ice suspended on a swing, decorated with flowers. The song was a Birdsong Radio anthem and a big favourite of the Queen's.

Just as the entertainment drew to a close, the Queen cocked her head to one side. She could hear something over the wall in the square.

"Listen!" Dance music filtered through the air. "I think the party has started."

The Queen led her guests onto the arched belvedere overlooking Pembridge Square to join in the revelry. Party in the Square, a free open-air disco, had been arranged by the kingdom's most celebrated club entrepreneur Monsieur Marais. Invitations to attend had been extended to all residents of Pembridge.

Monsieur Marais, a kestrel of French descent, was quite a character and, unlike his name, had a dry sense of humour. Whenever he went flying, he wore a floppy-eared hat. His eyry, The Cupola - a former crow's nest that looked to the eye like an overturned tea bowl on a saucer - nestled on an upper branch of the mighty oak tree on the River Brae's northern bank, between Pembridge Town and Willow Twine. It was one of the grandest nests in the area, with uninterrupted views of the river.

For all his wealth and success, Monsieur Marais was an elusive character. He much preferred the quieter pursuits of life, such as kite flying and collecting valuable antique falcon eggs. His famous 'fierce and rulin'' outdoor nightclub, appropriately named Imaginarium, had seen many competitors off and was a clubbers paradise for young birds and bees.

Loud dance music punctured the air as laser beams, like flickering firecrackers, danced across the evening sky, lighting up the party animals dancing below. Even the Wall of Gabbling Gargoyles joined in with the celebrations, singing along to the tunes.

"Feel the vibe," motioned the Queen as she recklessly threw her forelegs into the air, embracing the rhythm of the beat. "Can you feel it!"

Perched upon a jutting pediment, staying very much in the shadows, was Madame Petronella keeping a close eye on the goings-on. Although she would never have owned up to eavesdropping, her highly tuned ears couldn't help but catch a waft of conversation between Lady Muck and Dawlok. "Remember the codename, Operation Oak."

It transpired, Lady Muck had devised a secret sting in the tail, to have Mike killed that very evening during his return journey home. Dawlok had been recruited to execute the plot.

It was ten past the hour of nine and time for Mike and his cohorts to bid the Queen and her guest's farewell and head back home. Mike packed his red tail and skateboard into his backpack, lifted Wriggler into the pouch, and put the bag on over his jacket.

"Toodle-pip!" Wriggler called out to Pip, with a big grin on his face.

"I've decided to join you," announced Pip, sounding rather pleased with her decision. "I'm a bit bored of solitary living. I need a vacation, and where better to go than Portobello Creek. I hear there's a wonderful boatel there, moored on the river. I believe it's called the Houseboat!"

Grandfather Gus lifted his eyebrows in wonderment, not knowing whether to take Pip's last comment as a compliment or as a self-invited invitation. In the grand order of things, did it really matter who came along, thought Grandfather Gus? "There's always room for a houseguest," he concluded, jocularly, "as long as you don't overstay your welcome."

The Tail of 'Too Bad' Mike

CHAPTER 13

The Plot

The plot was simple; to eliminate 'Too Bad' Mike. How Dawlok would achieve this feat would include a fishing hook attached to string, a bedsheet weighted with stones, and two of the fiercest and meanest ruffians in the kingdom, the Bandit brothers. Grabit and Havit of the infamous Bandit family were known collectively as The Firm and descended from a long line of smash-and-grab robbers. To be blatantly honest, they were neither fierce nor mean; in fact, they were bundling idiots. Due to the Lord Chief Justice's rigorous policing policies, their days of operating on the wrong side of the law had long since gone.

Nowadays, the rat brothers worked legitimately as bouncers or personal security guards when they could find the work, which in Pembridge was rare. For them, Dawlok's proposal was a dream job and a pleasant reminder of the good old days. It was a once in a lifetime chance for them to honour their family's name of Bandit and revive their lost reputation as the kingdom's most fearless and despised villains.

"You'll be rewarded handsomely when the job is completed," Dawlok assured the Bandit brothers.

Lord and Lady Muck conceived the plot under much duress and in great haste without giving adequate attention to the finer details. That said, if the plan was accomplished, it would rid them of Mike forever. Clearly, the Mucks could not be seen to be involved. Their connection would be discreetly channelled through Dawlok, who was still officially on the Salazar payroll as the Tower's warder.

The plan was thus: remove a bedsheet from the royal laundry, tie the four corners together, weight it with stones, winch Mike off the raft on the end of a hook, entangle him in the weighted sheet and toss him ruthlessly into the depths of the River Brae to drown.

"Caught, hook, line, and sinker," were the final words on the matter by Lady Muck.

Just as the nightingale's melody drifted from the castle turret signalling nightfall was fast approaching; and just as the moon had switched on every light bulb in its complicated circuitry; Mike, Wriggler, Grandfather Gus, Mr Stitch, Pip, and the dithering Carrier pigeon set off from Hive Castle on their short trek to join Harvey at Pembridge jetty.

No sooner had they bid their farewells and departed than Dawlok and his pair of sidekicks headed off carrying their bag of tricks. They chose an alternative route that would bring them out further along the riverbank, where the mighty oak tree stands and home to Monsieur Marais.

Madame Petronella's earlier suspicions had been rightly aroused, for no sooner did Dawlok leave than the owl flew silently overhead in hot pursuit.

Dawlok knew he had one chance of executing the plot, and only one. As the raft passed under the overhanging branches of the majestic oak tree, he and his two cohorts would be strategically positioned and ready to pounce. He also understood that coordination would be vital to prevent anyone on the raft from realising what was happening.

Around twenty minutes later, Dawlok and his two heavies arrived at the mighty oak by the river. A gentle evening mist covered the water. Still on their trail, circling high above flew Madame Petronella.

"When I see the raft approaching, I'll hoot three times like an owl," Dawlok hissed at the Bandit brothers. "That's your signal to pounce."

"Okay, guv'nor ... Owl's the word," confirmed Grabit. The two ruffians nodded their understanding and then climbed somewhat awkwardly up the side of the tree trunk onto one of the lower branches of the tree. When they were positioned, Dawlok passed the tied bedsheet and fishing hook up to them, followed by several pebbles from the riverbank.

"Don't forget the signal," repeated Dawlok. "Three hoots."

Dawlok clambered up the trunk and positioned himself on another branch higher up the tree, with an uninterrupted view along the river. Once Dawlok and the Bandit brothers had settled, Petronella, the owl, landed discreetly on the highest branch of the tree, from where she could observe and listen to every word spoken. There they all sat and waited.

Unbeknown to Dawlok, to help kill time, his two accomplices were steadily becoming rat-faced. Having already drunk copious amounts of free nectar ale that afternoon at the summer fête, they'd now decided to swig more, from ale bottles they'd concealed inside their coat pockets.

"Great little pub, The Oak," joked Grabit.

Havit almost split his coat sides laughing.

Meanwhile, Dawlok continued to peer attentively through his binoculars, watching for any sign of activity on the river. He didn't have long to wait. In the distance, he saw a blue-sailed raft approaching.

"Too-wit too-woo, too-wit too-woo, too-wit too-woo," came forth an owl's call.

A look of surprise flashed across Dawlok's face.

Unbeknown to the Bandit brothers, it was Petronella that hooted, not Dawlok.

"Let 'em have it, Grabit," called out Havit.

In a panic, Grabit dropped his ale bottle and randomly swung the fishing hook into the air. In doing so, the hook caught Dawlok's jacket and hoisted him off the upper branch he was sitting on. Before Grabit had time to comprehend what was happening, the hook ripped through Dawlok's jacket and sent him toppling down on top of Havit. In the mad scuffle that followed, Dawlok became entangled in the weighted sheet Havit was holding and tumbled out of the tree, pulling Havit and Grabit with him. The sheet became caught in a branch overhanging the river as the Bandit brothers fell into the water below.

Never before had a plan so spectacularly backfired. The Bandit brother's stupidity had bedevilled the Mucks plot.

"Iceberg ahead," squawked the lookout, frantically, from the crow's nest atop the mast on Grandfather Gus's raft. The dithering Carrier pigeon ruffled its feathers in trepidation. Having just woken from a quick nap, he hadn't yet fully taken command of all his senses. As such, he failed to identify precisely what it was that was towering up from the water directly ahead.

"I knew you should never have christened this raft *Titanic*, Grandad."

"This is no time for hindsight, junior," declared Grandfather Gus, gruffly.

"We're fated," moaned Wriggler, anxiously. "What am I to do? I can't swim!"

Everyone on board strained their eyes in the subdued light to try and distinguish the outline of the iceberg.

"All paws on deck," ordered Captain Gus as he pulled hard on the line attached to the sail to alter course, but no matter how hard he tugged, the sail seemed not to want to move. The menacing iceberg approached with alarming speed.

In a final attempt to slow the raft down, the Captain called out to Harvey, "let go of the string." Harvey hadn't heard the pigeon's warning, nor did he hear Grandfather Gus, so he had no idea they were heading for a collision.

"I thought you were supposed to be on watch, not sleeping!" Captain Gus shouted up to the crow's nest. "You pigeon-toed goof!"

The pigeon took exception to the remark, an expression he considered to be disrespectful. "I was only having a nap," he cooed as if to excuse his incompetence, and then complained, "there are only so many things you can do, and then you don't. Anyway, you never gave me any binoculars."

Looming perilously ahead, the mountainous iceberg drew closer and closer with every second until...

"CRASH..."

Titanic collided sideways with the iceberg ripping driftwood from its starboard side. Everyone aboard fell backward as the vessel came to a sudden, shuddering halt and began to tilt perilously to the fore, sending water lapping on deck and into the biscuit tin.

The impact caused the string attaching Harvey to the raft to untie. In the confusion that followed, Harvey disappeared beneath the cold, murky water. Wreckage was strewn everywhere.

"Pigeon overboard," shrieked the pigeon as he promptly abandoned ship and flew off towards the nearby oak tree. He landed on an upper branch that coincidently turned out to be the same branch Madame Petronella was perched on.

The owl turned her head, rather nonchalantly, fixing her piercing black eyes upon the new arrival.

"Not you again!" she hooted impertinently. "Will I never escape your sight?"

The pigeon was most put out by the owl's indignant and unwelcoming behaviour.

"I have as much right to perch here as you have," he declared with gusto. "Besides, I'm a shipwreck survivor. I should be taken pity on."

The owl was having none of that and promptly corrected the pigeon. "Shouldn't that be, 'jumped ship'?"

The pigeon looked mightily ruffled by her caustic remark.

"I have no idea what you're implying ... I'll have you know, my great-great-great-great uncle worked on secret reconnaissance missions in World War II, and ..."

"Yes, yes," interrupted the owl, "I've heard all that before. Lest you hadn't realised, I saw exactly what happened down on the river below."

"Well, if you must know, I was catching up on a nap I misplaced earlier in the day," explained the pigeon, with a smidgeon of sarcasm in his voice.

"A disaster is unfolding before your eyes, the likes of which will go down in history, and all you can think to do is take a snooze!" said the owl incredulously. "What about relaying a Morse code?"

"I'm prone to falling asleep without warning. It hits me out of the blue, and when it happens, I don't even know I'm doing it. The condition is called nappingitis. Doctors know only one cure for it, waking tablets," explained the pigeon. "I'm just not very good at taking tablets."

"Well, that's news to me," decided the wise owl.

"And what's a Morse code?" asked the pigeon, flippantly.

"Just forget I ever mentioned it," answered the owl, dismissively.

"There's no need to be so rude..." cooed the pigeon under his breath.

At that moment, Monsieur Marais, having not long returned from the Party in the Square, poked his beak out of his eyry to see what all the noise was. He did not look in a happy mood.

"*Pouvez-vous baisser la voix tous les deux? J'ai eu une journée bien remplie et j'essaye de dormir,*"[1] and with that, he disappeared back indoors.

"A cup of tea would have been nice," mumbled the pigeon under his breath.

The owl dismissed the pigeon's last remark and continued to watch the developing drama occurring onboard the *Titanic*.

"Lower the dinghy," instructed Captain Gus, who'd taken on an air of deadpan seriousness that could

---

[1] English translation: "Can you two keep your voices down? I've had a busy day and I'm trying to sleep."

have easily won him an Oscar nomination.

"What dinghy?" yelled Mike, looking bewildered by his grandad's command.

"This ... inflatable," demonstrated the Captain, as he yanked it out from under a seat, then pulled the air ring, and watched it inflate.

Behind the raft, still shadowing the evening's fading light, floated the terrifying iceberg.

As *Titanic* listed to the fore, with water lapping upon its deck, Mike lowered the dinghy into the river.

"Sorry to take the wind out of your sail, Captain," pointed out Mr Stitch, just as the mast snapped and collapsed overboard, "we're sinking."

"Abandon ship," called out Captain Gus. "Abandon ship."

CHAPTER 14

Pineapple Rings

Mike, Wriggler, Grandfather Gus, Pip, and Mr Stitch watched in silence from the inflatable as *Titanic* broke up and sank to the depths of the river.

And there they remained, perfectly still, as if to take in the enormity of the situation and their lucky escape.

"I don't suppose anyone has any paddles?" Mr Stitch broke the temporary lull.

"No," replied Grandfather Gus, abruptly.

In the calmness of the night, the dinghy drifted aimlessly in no particular direction.

A few minutes later, Pip piped up, "Shame about Harvey." She'd remained quiet throughout the whole drama, having never sailed on the river before. "He seemed like a good old soul ... in a funny kind of way."

"If I know Harvey," injected Mr Stitch, as if to try and lighten the mood a little, "he's probably snoozing on the great riverbed up in the heavens."

"Harvey," Mike called up into the dark, chilly sky, "we'll miss you."

The survivors huddled together in the dinghy to keep themselves warm while silently wondering if and when rescue would ever arrive.

Sometime later, deep in the middle of the night, something peculiar happened. On the surface of the water, a series of ripples appeared. Everyone in the dinghy cast their gaze expectantly upon them and wondered where they were coming from. As if by providence, but clearly it wasn't, in the midst of the swell out popped a head … Harvey's.

No one could believe their eyes. Attached around Harvey's body was a bright yellow pineapple ring.

"Don't even go there," warned Harvey, as he swam, a little unstably, towards the dinghy.

Mike knew Harvey could be a bit tetchy at times, so he chose his words tactfully.

"We thought you were dead," well, not that tactfully, and then proceeded to ask, "Why have you got a pineapple ring around you?"

"Humans!" carped Harvey, crossly. "Picnickers on the riverbank, no doubt … chucking their garbage into the river … as you can see, I appear to have become rather attached to a piece!" Harvey was clearly in no mood for jokes.

"The trash that gets thrown into this river," he complained, as several other pineapple rings rose to the surface of the water. "You wouldn't believe it."

"Not looking where you were going, eh!" wondered Mr Stitch, who knew how nosey Harvey could be at times.

"Laugh if you must," Harvey defended himself. "It's rude to mock the afflicted."

"Can you remove it, or is it stuck?" asked Grandfather Gus, referring to the pineapple ring.

"Stuck," snapped Harvey.

"So we see," grinned Wriggler, who was fascinated by it all.

"No doubt it will become unattached at some point in time," assured Mr Stitch.

"We were expecting the *Carpathia* to turn up and rescue us," said Grandfather Gus, "not a trout."

Harvey had never heard of the *Carpathia*, so he had no idea what Grandfather Gus was going on about.

"Now you're back in the water of the living, can you tug us back home?" asked Grandfather Gus, sounding relieved assistance had finally arrived.

Harvey swam alongside the dinghy. Mr Stitch leaned out and grabbed the string that was still attached to Harvey's body.

"Time we were heading home," announced Mr Stitch, as he tied the string securely through a small ring on the dinghy. Grandfather Gus agreed, as did Wriggler, who was beginning to feel mightily tired, having not slept a wink all day.

"I think we've had enough excitement for one day," decided Grandfather Gus, as he prepared to set sail.

Harvey gently tugged the string.

"Dessert is on you, Harvey," Grandfather Gus jested, as the dinghy slowly pulled away.

"You always come up trumps, Grandad."

And with that, Grandfather Gus let rip the mightiest fart he'd done all day that propelled the dinghy down the river faster than a skimming heron homeward bound.

However, unbeknown to everyone aboard, Boreas the wind had been keeping a watchful eye overhead, and it was under his gentle influence that the dinghy finally made it home.

As they approached the sweeping bend at Willow Twine, a wondrous sight greeted them. Hanging from the branches of the willow trees were lines of brightly coloured bunting. Along the riverbank, rows of glow worms flickered like tea lights. Gantree and his fellow willows had spent the afternoon decorating their limbs to welcome everyone back and used the fabric swatches Mr Stitch had left in the wicker basket outside his shop.

Just as Wriggler curled up inside his favourite wormhole; and just as Mr Stitch knuckled down for the night at the Holt; just as Grandfather Gus snuggled up in his swaying hammock; and just as Pip huddled down in the corner of the canopy overhanging Grandfather Gus's hammock; just as Harvey bedded in for the night on the riverbed; and just as Mike arrived outside his burrow in Colville Hollow, a raindrop fell upon the River Brae, and then a second and then a third. Up in the moonlit sky, a cloudburst opened, and the rain came bucketing down all across the kingdom of Pembridge, just as Boreas had promised.

Mike removed his tail and washed it in a bowl of warm soapy water before laying it neatly upon the wicker tray to dry.

It was time for bed. He was so exhausted he could barely keep his eyes open. As he reached inside the top drawer of the matchbox chest and pulled out a nightshirt, his paw went straight through Clive the spider's latest intricate web, the one he'd spent all day spinning.

Clive poked his head out of the drawer, fully expecting to see a scrumptious meal trapped inside his snare.

"Clive," a look of surprise flashed across Mike's face.

"You're back," retorted Clive, looking greatly miffed to discover there was no tasty insect for him to gorge on.

"With tail intact!" announced Mike.

"So I see," said Clive.

"And what a day it's been," Mike confessed, as he fell on top of the feather duvet on his bed. "You wouldn't believe what happened to me today."

"I don't suppose I would," agreed Clive. He clearly had other things on his mind as he closely surveyed the damage Mike had inflicted upon his expertly spun web. "You wouldn't believe how many hours I spent today spinning this web only to have you arrive and put your paw through it."

"No … I don't suppose I would," yawned Mike, louder than a chorus of hibernating caterpillars. "You're always working on that web."

"It's not just any web," Clive corrected Mike. "It's a world wide web."

"I've been to the Tower of the Winds," mumbled Mike, sleepily, "and back."

This news came as no surprise to Clive. "Hopefully, now that you've found your tail, things can return to some normality around this place."

Mike rolled over on one side and pulled the duvet over him.

"I'll have you know," declared Clive, with a clear ring in his tone, as if he was about to commence a rant of epic proportions.

"ZzzzzzzZZzzzzzzz," the drifting melody of a soothing snore rose from Mike's bed, drowning out Clive's words.

"You can't get off the hook that easy…" Clive huffed on and on for what must have been a goodly length of time.

Mike never heard a single word of Clive's rant, for he had fallen into a deep, calming sleep.

Finally, at the end of Clive's tirade, he surveyed the broken web one last time before concluding, "I suppose I could always spin another one. Maybe try a new design … it'll give me something to do tomorrow." And with that, Clive, the spider, disappeared back inside the dark recess of the top drawer, and life regained its natural tranquillity.

And so it came to pass in the vastness of evermore; Mike entered the journals of history and became known to all as 'Too Bad' Mike, Wriggler revealed he had another, less selfish side to his personality, and Grandfather Gus discovered he had a secret female admirer. That night the kingdom of Pembridge fell asleep a far safer and happier place to live than it had been at the beginning of the day.

An extract from the front page of the following days *Pembridge Times,* under the headline *'Titanic Sinks,'* reported:

"A weighted bedsheet, as white as fresh 'snow on a raven's back,'[2] was found dangling from an overhanging branch of the mighty oak tree alongside the River Brae close to where this horrendous disaster occurred. Rather oddly, entangled in the sheet was the warder of the Tower of the Winds. Quite what he was doing there has yet to be established. It would seem the *Titanic* careered into the sheet, damaging the vessel, after which it sank. Two further, somewhat inebriated, survivors were found floating in the river clinging to a pineapple ring. Their identities have yet to be released. *Titanic* debris covers a wide area. All survivors have now returned safely to their homes."

---

[2] William Shakespeare: *Romeo and Juliet* (3.2.19)

To be continued …

Book II in the *'Too Bad' Mike* series:

'Too Bad' Mike and

Turquoise Island Rocket Factory

The Tail of 'Too Bad' Mike

ISBN 978-1-916-14655-6

The Tail of 'Too Bad' Mike

Printed in Great Britain
by Amazon